ANGELS CHÎC

ANGELS CHÎC

A novel of fantastic adventure

Arjuna Krishna-Das

Atma Communications

Published in Great Britain and the USA
by Atma Communications, 2008

Atma Communications
London, England
www.atma-communications.com

ISBN 978-0-9559112-0-0

British Library Cataloguing in Publication Data:
A catalogue record for this book is
available from the British Library

Printed and bound by
Lightning Source, England and USA

This book is dedicated to
His Grace Krishna-Ksetra Prabhu

CONTENTS

PART TWO
SELENE **113**

PART THREE
SUNDANCE **247**

Acknowledgements

I would like to thank the following friends, who have all contributed something special to this book: Daevid Allen (for permission to quote his lyrics), Titiksu dasa and Swami Suryananda (for spiritual inspiration), Joyce E Kerr (who co-authored a few pages about Robert), A.C. Bhaktivedanta Swami Prabhupada (for spiritual inspiration and quotations from his *Brahma Samita*, *Krishna Book* and *Srimad Bhagavatam*), my mum Rosalind Werner (for everything, especially the proof-reading), and all the members of the Rose Lane Writers Workshop, Liverpool, 1988-92.

ARJUNA KRISHNA-DAS

She is the mother of everything,

And you   are   her   egg.

To pass beyond the countless worlds...

The eternal wheel...

The ceaseless tides of selves...

Ever passing away, before our eyes...

Gong – Angels Egg

ARJUNA KRISHNA-DAS

Pr O logue

Vishnu lolls back easily on the hill. He supports it all; it's good to pass time here. His form is magnificent, with a shine of its own illuminating all around. His face exhudes a radiant calmness. His eyes shine blue, His beehive-shaped crown, gold, with a miniature fan of precious stones adorning its peak.

A pink blossom-flower falls from a tree onto his light blue, muscular but hairless chest. He moves His lower right hand and brushes it away with a rod of twisted gold stems, onto the soft fragrant grass beside him. His upper right hand holds a lotus flower, the left, a conch shell and flashing disc.

Garlands of flowers hang round His neck down to a garment of red and gold wrapping him an inch below the navel. He feels the season around him. *Kali-Yuga* – or winter – is coming. There is a fresh bite to the air; clouds and moods of dark grey and blue fluff the sky. Soon the thick clumps of trees surrounding, above and down the valley will drop the last of their leaves. He hears the music of the brook trickle splashfully at His side. A small fish struggles just beneath the water's surface; it is swimming upstream. As the current rises and falls, it flounders on a rock. Vishnu looks at it and smiles. From Pisces – he blinks his eyes

*   *   *

The couple held hands. There was nothing else to hold on to. They looked out of their visors onto a freshly unseen pattern. They, in their glinting 'white' space suits appeared to be travelling at c, the speed of light. Their mass was normal. The woman spoke. "I can't stop crying. Let me die like this"

The man could feel tears welling up in him too. He moved a free arm and glanced at the strapless watch glued to his slightly larger suit. A line of text ran up jointed sections of its arm – United States of America – NASA – Apollo 23. He turned and tugged her arm until she looked at him. "We've been going for half an hour now".

"I'm not sure what that means anymore," she managed, between sobs. "It's all lit up. We're Here!"

"I know. It's incredible. Let's get back though. We can come again." He spoke to the command system. "All stop. Confirm stop." Instantly the stars were stilled around them. They were both closely aware of the sounds of each other breathing fast through the suit radios and it comforted them. He waited a moment. "Prepare to jump. Confirm..."

"Going somewhere?" asked the figure suddenly materialised before them. Their mouths opened in astonishment. Here was a man who dropped in unannounced, light hours from anywhere, spoke their radio wavelength and managed to traverse deep space in nothing but a shirt, tie, dark trousers and shoes, a thick trench coat. He shifted his elderly, heavy set look, slowly glancing between them.

"Location – Homelab – Liverpool – Earth.

"Ah." He looked relieved. "May I join you?" Without waiting for an answer he went on. "You're wondering where my space suit is, whether I'm an apparition, a hallucination, god, ghost – that sort of thing. No, it's perfectly simple if you have a little imagination. I'm travelling in a projected air cube. Why didn't you think of that? Would have saved a lot of time and trouble in Florida, stealing those antiques you call space suits. Take your helmets off if you like. Your air must be getting stale by now."

"Whoever you are, I don't think we should do that" said the man.

The woman spoke. "We hardly know you."

The figure shrugged. "As you like. I can't blame you for being cautious. Shall we go in for some fresh air? I can hardly negotiate like this."

The man in the space suit closed his eyes and gripped the woman's hand harder through their thick gloves. "Confirm prepare jump. Confirm Homelab. Jump confirm jump."

Opening them again he could see the familiar room. Sudden changes of scene always unnerved him. He reached up and unclasped his helmet as his companion did. The old man in the trench coat still stood before them, hands clasped together.

"May you both come to live as long as I." he said, bowing slightly. "We have business to discuss. A favourable trade for both parties. Allow me to prepare some refreshments while you change". He left by the door; they could hear him walk down the stairs.

ARJUNA KRISHNA-DAS

PART ONE
ENCHANTMENT

1   Steam Rolled

If only they'd all go away, thought Jane tiredly, climb aboard some sort of ark and sail off into the middle of the Irish Sea, never to be seen again, never to ask me another question, never to reproduce.

Turning her head, she noticed that she had passed the autobank a block ago, and retraced her steps. The machine was quiet, polite and gullible, seemingly as ignorant of Jane's bank balance as she preferred to be. A little further on, she paused inside The Health Store for bags of organic potatoes, tomatoes and a packet of rennet-free cheddar.

"It must be lovely working here," she remarked to the born-again hippy sitting behind the counter. He smiled and looked down to twiddle his 'Kill the car' enamel badge.

"It should be. It really should. That's why I opened. To serve the local community with an alternative. An alternative to pre-packaged processed instant dead animal crap."

"Right on!" Jane nodded.

"Trouble is, they're all brainwashed. They love eating rubbish. One look at the price of eco-friendly, cruelty-free toothpaste and they bomb off down to Kwik-Save. Don't care if they're full of cancer by forty."

"We have to work at it bit by bit."

"True, very true. You do meet some lovely people – look at the noticeboard – and you can read a lot. I'm Dave, by the way."

"Jane". For a moment, as cash changed hands, they exchanged a smiley twinkle, a little buzz of friendly amusement. "See ya."

"Tara."

It was nearly six. Time for tea and a smoke. Time to visit Mo. Mo did nice sixteenths, nice eighths and nice quarters. Jane felt she deserved a nice 'teenth after her hellish day. A day of staying calm, of patience, of self-control well beyond any normal conception of duty.

The dusty dual carriageway lost its garish bars, its newsagents, its fruit, veg and junk shops. Elegant Georgian terraces rose on one side, back from the road facing the Park. It curved at an aesthetically pleasing angle while Jane's hair danced in the March gusts. Presently she crossed over and climbed the steps to Mo's front door, ringing the bell while inhaling the sweet aroma of incense blended with fine Turkish hashish.

The door opened. "Come in. How are you? Great. Can I just leave you in here for a minute?" Jane was filed effortlessly into the front room, and plumped herself down on a cushion by the rocking horse. She removed her jacket and laid it down beside her, fishing in a pocket for Silk Cut, skins and Zippo. Emma and Jake were there, also a dishevelled scarecrow with peroxide dreadlocks who passed her a joint. Wild, pulsating, African rhythms oozed quietly from a large mongrel seventies hi-fi system. The room was large, but full of things; plants hanging all over the dusty windows, cushions, rugs, shelves, ornaments, paraphernalia, the odd mattress, an occasional hookah. 'The Pot Shop' announced a sign leaning on top of the fireplace. A rug-sized piece of material printed with Indian designs dangled from the ceiling. It had been slit to fit around the light flex, giving it the appearance of a massive yoni.

"How are youse doing ?", enquired Jane of Emma and Jake.

"Oh, all right" replied Emma. "I fixed the brakes on the van today, so we're off to Wales soon. Pete said we could stay at his; chill out for a bit."

"I can't see that methane generator getting going in a hurry" remarked Jane.

"Well, he's got enough incentive to do something about it" pointed out Jake. "About a ton in fact." Jane passed the joint. Brave little beams of evening sunlight struggled through the atmosphere to play on a montage of Krishna pictures opposite the window. "How are you?"

"Fine. Nothing a nervous breakdown or total amnesia wouldn't put right."

"Work bad?"

"Work very, very bad." Jane stuck her tongue out. "Should be kept for people so bored they go fishing and watch TV." She said this unselfconsciously, despite being the possessor of a warm and tranquillising 22" G.E.C. model herself, often used to view unwholesome late night movies. "Or born-again Christians." she added, maliciously and unnecessarily.

"What is it you do?" asked the scarecrow.

"I'm a social worker dealing with extremely disturbed adolescents." The company nodded, scratched their necks, gazed at the rug and reached for stash boxes sympathetically. Jake turned the tape over.

"Tea?!?" enquired a grinning Mo appearing through the fronds of the doorway with tray in hands.

"Yes please." they chorused, nodding as she poured and handed out. Kitchen visitors had evidently left or were now making themselves comfortably at home.

"Gorgeous day, isn't it?" said Mo. "We went for a picnic in the park before. Lost half a pipe in the wind, but never mind, it was hot."

"Yeah." agreed Jane. "Due for another greenhouse summer no doubt. Could I trouble you for a 'teenth?"

"You could indeed" replied Mo, producing a half-melon of hash, heavy knife and scales. "Anyone else?" Anyone else wanted some too, so she got down to the business, carving accurately, moving crumbs from pan to pan with expert precision, and distributing to each their allotted share. Spliffs spread, minds meandered and Jane's troubles left for some fresh air. Eventually she did too, returning moments later for her shopping.

Feeling light as a cloud, she negotiated the park and made her way home. Inserting the key in her front door, she weighed the arguments for and against going for a pizza instead of cooking. Oh well, she thought. I'll just lob it all in the wok and wave it about a bit. No more walking tonight. Just me and Joni Mitchell. And the situations vacant in Community Care, she mused as an afterthought.

Jane's flat was simply, comfortable. She had acquired the tenancy through a complex web of friends, acquaintances, deceit, blackmail, and, as always required when successful in the murky world of rented accommodation, a large degree of luck (or good karma, depending on your philosophical standpoint). The kitchen, her first stop, was decorated in bright clean primaries, and looked out onto an attractive jungle, cats' playground, or raspberry and nettle nursery, again depending on your point of view. One day she planned to do a bit of 'guerrilla farming' which she had read about in Green Anarchist as being a terribly right-on self-sufficient sort of subversive activity. Never mind if Carol and Jo downstairs would probably be only too delighted for someone to scythe through the trifid-like growth obscuring their view. She would do it secretly. One day. She could even stop supporting the military-industrial police-state complex by going on the dole. Once her overdraft was sorted out perhaps.

For the moment though, she cooked her hard-earned food beautifully, then settled down to a relaxing evening, eating, reading and getting stoned to some good music. Later she woke feeling cold and bleary. 'Too much!' she thought, smiling and stretching and tumbling off the sofa all at once. Fumbling, switching lights and clocks, she stumbled into bed, dead to the world.

*   *   *

"di-di-di-di   di-di-di-di   di-di-di-di   di-di-di-di" whispered the alarm clock. It cleared its throat and tried again. "Di-Di-Di-Di   Di-Di-Di-Di   Di-Di-Di-Di   Di-Di-Di-Di". Impatiently it shouted "DI-DI-DI-DI-DI-DI-DI-DI-DI-DI-DI-DI-DI- DI-D!". Jane crossed the room in a sprint and pressed the little green 'off' button. She raised her head and yawned. What a dream! If only she could remember it better. Her nipples were still hard from his touch, her body feeling lithe and sexy.

Only an hour left to be herself, in her own cosy world then it would begin. Why her? she wondered. What had she done to deserve this daily torment? Pulling herself together, she tried to think of the good side of Emlyn House – the camaraderie, the business and excitement and unpredictability. Sometimes she felt happy to be helping young souls and loved them for their unpretentiousness, or humour, or pathetic vulnerability. More usually, however, feelings of doom and fear were more prominent. She showered quickly, tied up her hair and dressed in jeans and a paisley shirt. Taking her jacket and mirror bag she set off in a whirl. There was no need to make sandwiches for lunch, for one of the occupational hazards of residential social work is weight gain. Emlyn's meals were no exception.

As her flat metaphorically sighed, closed its eyes and went back to sleep, Jane strode the route to work swiftly under budding trees, bursting with new life and birdsong. On the way she bought some cigarettes and a Daily Post from Mohammed's. In minutes she arrived. Carol made coffee while they woke up to change-over meeting in the lounge. Jane luxuriated in a deep armchair and tried to focus on Steve's nocturnal news. Carol, plump and maternal, asked a great number of questions, commenting perceptively. George sat near the edge of his chair joining in and taking notes, while Tony seemed to take as much comfort hiding behind his beard and glasses (eyes down, nodding) as Jane did in her womb-cloud. After twenty minutes Steve rose, announcing his great desire for imminent slumber, and the meeting finished. Jane sat blinking, mentally putting on her real work clothes – a suit of armour.

The early shift were now aware of their incumbent charges' activities during the past sixteen hours: One minor scrap, two hyperactive suspected amphetamine users, one out half the night, two moody and depressed, four fairly happy, and a new arrival. John had been bailed out and delivered at four this morning by the police after his latest breaking and entering spree, disowned by his mother, unable to cope. 'Nobody ever takes them off us when we can't cope' thought Jane uncharitably. Actually this was untrue. There was always borstal.

The men went upstairs to call down to breakfast those boys able to get up while Carol fried and Jane laid out the cornflakes etcetera. They all breakfasted together noisily.

Afterwards Jane shut herself away in the lavatory. A tear tricked down her nose. She sniffled. There was no-one to replace her if she went home sick. She had to go on. Washing her face and putting on half a smile, she returned to the dining room, volunteering to look after John. Tony said he would phone schools and schemes with excuses for the bedridden, then tidy rooms. George had some paperwork to do and offered to 'float', helping with whatever needed to be done, while Carol cooked lunch, perhaps showing someone how to make a casserole.

The home was a large detached Victorian residence, surrounded by chestnut trees and with its own driveway away from the wide but quiet road. Four stories high, it had been built as a symbol of elegant opulence at the zenith of the City's shipping trade. A black fire escape made its way down one side, and a well-blended extension jutted into the garden. In a room on the second floor over the front porch the sunlight slowly moved down over a sleeping cherub's face. His eyes and nose twitched and he seemed to mumble something. His short, shaved hair was black. As he muttered, his hands fumbled with the duvet and most of it slid to the floor. He was wearing red football shorts over a pasty white body, thin, small and almost hairless. Jane's figure appeared at the door. She shut it and left him to lie in a little longer. Later she went in again and called his name until he awoke. Asking him to wash and dress then come downstairs, she left again.

As she looked over the police report one more time, John walked into the lounge and sat down in a chair opposite her. "All right la?", he ventured, giving her an apprehensive glance then looking away.

"Hello John", she replied, "I'm Jane. I'm going to help take care of you while you're away from your mum. Do you know why you're here?" Apparently he didn't. "You've been caught breaking into a house again." D'you know why you did it?" John stared at a mains socket intensely. "Was it for the excitement? ". His eyes lit up. "OK, what else is exciting to do?"

"Skateboardin' ", he said at last.

"Have you got a skateboard ?" she asked.

"Yeah."

"What's it like ?"

"Fast."

"Don't you ever fall off?". He thought for a moment then shook his head. "Would you like me to get your skateboard for you?"

"When can I go home?" Now Jane looked down and thought.

"I don't know. It's up to you and your mum. You mainly. You've got to go to school every day. It's only another year. Stay out of trouble and make some new friends. You're sharing a room with Lee. Get to know him later. You'll like him." Stoney-eyed, John gave little further information about himself or his family that morning, and sighed with relief when Jane left him alone at last. Jane herself relaxed, and, making herself another coffee, started to write him up.

A hearty lunch later, the afternoon wearing on, Jane worked away, far away in her head. She saw to things, talked to people, operated the word processor and the phone. Her morning energy had worn off, and she lost herself in daydreams. Kissing bronzed athletes on tropical islands, water skiing, singing her songs on a World tour, New Age visionary in a post-industrial village.

'How utterly pathetic', she chided herself. 'Why don't you ever do anything to make these dreams come true?' It was true. She didn't. But at least she dreamt.

John would be OK. He was settling in already, making friends, surviving. That was his talent anyway. It was four. Thanking an unknown and unnamed God under her breath, Jane left, striding away, breathing the sweet, clean air of outside.

2   THE RADIO'NT

The fans whirred lazily. Silhouettes of leafy plants stood out amongst venetian stripes patterning a light grey oatmeal carpet. Here and there grew desks, cabinets and bookcases of deep stained mahogany. Tall lamps illuminated the scene through twisting leaves of stainless steel. In one area a short putting course was laid out, and on every desk stood computer equipment of the latest vintage. At one station sat a lone figure, glazed, deep in concentration.

Robert pondered. How could he hope to come up with a coherent hypothesis for the physical laws of a higher dimension? Tricky. Very tricky. The first steps might involve defining a one- or no-dimensional universe and working from there, he mused, looking out through mirror-tinted windows onto the Science Park's immaculate lawn. Rapidly his fingers moved across the terminal's keyboard, steadily and logically as the problem turned in his mind. The radio waves to be concealed were to consist of two perpendicular components – one wave of electric field – the other, an intersecting and complementary magnetic wave pattern. An antenna would be tuned in length to match a specific integer multiple of these beats, thus reflecting, trapping and amplifying the standing wave thereby obtained. Robert saw the koan in mechanical, physical, atomic terms. Part of a solution would clearly involve quantum (leap) aerial design.

He saw motes of dust dancing via multicoloured laser peaks, troughs of red, green, blue: snakes of the sub-electronic world.

"Hi Robert" called Josella. "How the hell are you? You're looking dreadful. What have you been up to? Come on, let's go for a drink."

"Oh Hi ! I've been working late. I was startled," replied Robert. Josella had walked across the office and put her hands on the back of his chair. She leaned forward.

"You're up to something Robert, I can tell. What's happening here on the screen?" As she pointed, their eyes turned. "What a weird and wonderful pattern!" she exclaimed. The intertwined sine waves were being panned by a simulated television camera of the Fujitsu's central processing unit – back, along, up, down, expanded, from a distance, from beside, a long way down.

"Incredible! I always knew you spent your time making beautiful patterns instead of working."

Robert was flustered. The tap of a key replaced his magical display with a simple 'Goodbye Robert' message. "Let's go for that drink. I'm celebrating a novel application of Liebeniz's third postulate in differential calculus."

Josella lowered her eyelashes, raised her chin and addressed him. "I see." Robert rose and put his jacket on. They walked out, extinguishing lights by touching personnel security until it lit green for both of them. Outside it was still warm as he unlocked the Cavalier from a few steps away. They climbed aboard, luxuriating in a cool blast from the air conditioning. The dashboard lit up and they pulled away, gliding across smooth tarmac, through the traffic lights and onto Wavertree Road. Remaining silent until pulling up at 'Ye Cracke', they sat drinking Bloody Marys and pints of Swan, talking shop and gossiping while the pub filled. They left at ten, back to their respective homes, beds and dreams.

*   *   *

Robert woke with a start. The room was embalmed in a warm pink hue as early sunlight strained to filter through the red curtains. He craned his neck to look at the still slumbering radio-alarm. His heart-beat slowly subsided; he hadn't slept in. The alarm wasn't due to go off for another hour. He willed himself return to oblivion, but strands of fear and loathing kept flooding his rapidly awakening mind. Damn! His body felt heavy. He needed more sleep.

The Arabian nightmare reassembled, remembered; he made a conscious effort to banish it.

Roisín returned to his thoughts as he turned over and moved into a comatose position, rearranging his pillows into a comfortable head mould. He remembered the pleasures of Ios, meeting her like that as she had coolly emerged from the water like a goddess, wearing only a blue G-string. She had sidled up to him and asked for a cigarette.

"I'm sorry, I don't smoke," he had replied, viewing her in rapture, drops of water glistening on her full and firm breasts.

29

"Marvellous, isn't it?" Gently intoxicated by sun and ouzo, he shifted his gaze over the shimmering Aegean.

"Yeah, sure is," she agreed, settling onto her hips and staring into the sunset. The silence was broken only by gentle waves lapping at the rocks. Long blonde hair was drying on her shoulders as she looked at him again, smiling that teasing smile. 'Sexy, arrogant, bitch...'

The alarm sounded again and he shifted from his semi-conscious state into one of semi-wakefulness, leaning over to turn the volume down. The birds were twittering outside, which filled him with a sense of irritation. Carefree birds, he thought and contemplated feeding them to Felix for breakfast. The creature opened its lazy green eyes and stared as he snatched a towel and stumbled into the shower. 'Ra!' The man was always in a hurry. From the bedroom, Robert could hear latest developments in Saudi Arabia. Canada was now sending three ships and eight hundred men. 'Why the Hell couldn't they get it together and take the bastard out with an SAS squad?' he thought, serving only to draw blood during his organised minute and a half shave. "Damn and blast," he snapped. This was not going to be a good day. Returning to his bedroom, he put on a white shirt, grey trousers and suitably anonymous tie.

Descending the stairs, he picked up the Telegraph and a small pile of windowed envelopes, placing them in his briefcase for later. He entered the kitchen and charmed Felix with a bowl of Whiskas, then fixed Weetabix and strong tea for himself. Passing admiring glances at the new Zanussi, pristine and white, he walked over to open the back door, and looked outside at the garden, inherited Floribunda bursting out by the far fence. He would have to cut the grass tonight, and resolved to let the mundane task relax him.

Saying goodbye to Felix and putting him outside, he reached for briefcase and light sports jacket, locked the door, and climbed into the car. He gunned the engine and shot out onto Brow Mount, a winding cul-de-sac of executive dwellings. Gateacre was just stirring into life now, and the traffic beginning to thicken along Woolton Road. Past the woods he drove, and past comfortably spaced bungalows, owners setting out for offices in BMWs, Jaguars and fashionably fast Fords. His elbow rested on the open window sill, fingers tapping to Art of Noise's 'Beatbox' CD.

Already he was yearning to log on and refine routines of the waveform modelling program. Never before had he committed himself so completely to a project. Nothing had ever challenged him so much. Only five years out of university, albeit post-graduate studies, the company had rewarded him well in both responsibility and remuneration. He now led a small team working on 'Stealth Communications', a highly speculative research project for the Ministry of Defence. There were rumours that a Middle Eastern state was sharing some of the enormous capital costs – for what return – Robert could only guess.

His proving years had been in the field of coding, creating algorithms to code and decode information securely, using largish prime numbers as keys. Now he had the near-impossible task of making the signals themselves invisible, coded or not. And, surprisingly, they were making progress. It was probably up a blind alley. He was realistic enough to know that, however, it was an interesting and untrodden path.

3   HEALTHY LOVE

Jane was in better spirits all round. She was refining her auto-pilot, and so far this week, work had passed without incident, accident or too much boredom. Dave definitely fancied her, and today, while the masses toiled (Bless Shifts), she would instigate a massive spring clean, and then, perhaps, nip out for another box of herb tea, completing her collection.

Careering through the flat she righted wrongs, watered drooping foliage, sorted linen, re-arranged, replaced, washed, hoovered and jettisoned. A new start, ready to turn dreams into... a newspaper at the bottom of her bag. She picked it out, made tea and lit a cigarette, then sat down to enjoy a break, unwilling to discard these unread words.

Deep in concentration, her teacup half-empty on the table beside her, Jane re-read the advertisement:

Liverpool Daily Post   Situations Vacant

SOCIAL WORKER/CARE ASSISTANT
GRADE 3/4
Applications are invited for the above post involving
all aspects of caring for patients with mental illness. A
CQSW and relevant experience would be an advantage
in this demanding and stimulating environment.
Ongoing training and exciting career development
opportunities will be provided in a progressive and
privately funded professional centre of excellence for
mental health.

Salary £10,334 - £16,423

Apply to Prof. E. Heisenberg,
Brookview Hospital, Aigburth Park, Liverpool 17
by 29th March 1990

A feeling of Déjà vu passed over her. She shut her eyes
and opened them again, focusing her attention on the closing
date for applications – today. Jane reached for her battered
typewriter. Go for it! she thought, progressive and privately
funded – bloody brilliant. Half an hour later she was on her
way to deliver the application personally. As she passed the
large and elegant villas of the bourgeois on the way down to
the river, her determination increased. This was it. Definitely.
The address was no letdown, with gorgeous views and well-
kept gardens. She didn't loiter. Exhilarated as the letter left
her hand, she spun round and headed back home. 'Might as

well drop in on Dave on my way back' she thought, intoxicated, invigorated, full of sunshine.

The shop was empty of people, full of tempting bottles, jars and cartons, smelt good. "Hi Dave," she called to the figure appearing from the back room.

He grinned. "Hi Jane. Good to see you."

She looked around and picked on a pack of jasmine tea. "This, please." She smiled back and placed a pound on the counter. "What'ya doin' this weekend?" Her smile crept into a grin.

"Nothing planned."

"Good."

They looked teasingly at each other and collapsed into laughter. Dave recovered first and took the initiative.

"How about a drink on Saturday night ?"

"On the ferry perhaps ?"

"Done," he agreed.

"What if I meet you here at seven and we'll catch a bus to the Pier Head. Or is that too early ?" continued Jane.

"Quarter past ?" enquired Dave, timidly.

"Right," agreed Jane. "until Saturday then. See you."

"Tara." They nodded, as friends caught in conspiracy, parting.

*   *   *

After a rather long drawn-out Friday, Saturday night finally dawned, or rather set. Jane set out for the evening looking good, despite having spent less time in the bathroom than most girls. She wasn't one to over-dabble with cosmetics, sources of supply tending to be limited to birthdays, Christmases and the

Animal Rights shop. In any case, it wouldn't do to dazzle Dave too much and make him feel shabby. Not that he was shabby exactly, more *organic*.

There he was waiting, looking at his watch through pebbly glasses and smoking a hand-rolled cigarette, actually looking very smart for one such as himself.

They greeted each other warmly, exchanging complements, then moved on to the bus stop outside Tesco. Just as it was contemplating raining, a bus arrived, picked them up and roared off towards town.

A short ride later they stepped off between Liver Building and Mersey. Dave bought tickets and they descended the enclosed walkway, passing local wildlife decked in colourful plumage, coming up.

A sharp wind caught them on the quayside. Jane pointed out the approaching ferry; Dave described the river's current state of ecological health.

"Did you go to Glastonbury this year?" he asked.

"Yes," replied Jane. "It was brilliant."

"I was selling earrings and Rizlas in the Green Field, by the sauna" he went on.

"A busman's holiday" she noted. "I hitched down in three lifts. One just up the M6 with two other girls, then one in an artic' with a divorced ex-teacher who'd set up his own trucking company, not having much luck with bank or dating agency. The last one was the best. Two guys in a Maestro – they worked in a power station, fixing things – took me right in via Cheddar Gorge. We drove up between the cliffs, got out and smoked a spliff. These little yellow men were abseiling down the rock, jumping from place to place. It was just beginning to rain then, too."

"Wow! Look, here's the ferry." They made for the boarding passage. When the procession of bodies and bikes had ended, a dock hand on the pier hauled up the gangplank and threw off ropes like tree trunks. It was getting dark. They found the bar and Jane bought two lagers, which they drank outside.

"It's very romantic out here, isn't it?" she said.

"Mmm. Do you do it much?"

"Constantly," she confided.

"Of course it's not the same as it was in ' 73."

"The river?"

"No – Glastonbury"

"I was only ... eight then."

"I was only thirteen. My parents took me."

"Wow. They were really together. You might have been called Moonstar or something."

"Would you?"

"What?"

"Call your baby Moonstar?"

"I'd probably call it all sorts of things. That sounds too much like monster. It would have to have an 'Off' switch anyway." She paused. "How's the shop?"

"Well, it's not too busy at the moment. Maybe people are still finishing off their Easter eggs. How's Emlyn House?"

"Awful, as usual. Bearable. I posted a job application on Thursday for something that looks really good. Mental health worker. Really well paid."

"I hope you get it."

"So do I. I'll go crazy if I don't do something soon.

A little something for Woodside?"

"I don't mind if I do." He inhaled deeply, bringing the joint to life, as Jane held out her lighter in clasped hands to him.

"Where are we going?" They looked over to the famous Liverpool waterfront, floodlit Liver buildings and Albert dock.

"Don't know. We could just stay here going round in triangles on the water."

"Sounds good," he murmured, passing the joint, which left an arm free to hold her. She snuggled up to him, leaning her head into his neck. They stayed that way for a long time, listening to the sounds of the river. The ferry docked and pushed off again. Dave bought another round of drinks.

"Thanks. What would you do if nothing could stop you?"

"Dave thought for a moment. "Grow my own organic veg. In a roof garden over the shop. Can't get much more local than that. Show it works and franchise the whole operation. Health Stores everywhere, all worked out in a conversion kit for pointed roofs."

"What is stopping you?"

"Oh nothing really, just time and money. What are you going to do if you grow up?"

"Me? Erm... travel the world and the seven seas ... live in a village weaving pots, teaching yoga ... sing."

"That doesn't sound too difficult. Made any plans?"

"Not yet. I just need to get my act together and save up a bit."

"Ahh." They looked out over the water, closely together for warmth, then slowly turned and kissed.

<u>4</u>   A HOME BY THE RIVER

Professor Heisenberg kept lifting things up from his desk and putting them down again. He couldn't understand how a pair of glasses could just vanish. For the third time he picked up a pile of magazines – Journal of Experimental Psychiatry – felt underneath and put them back. He swept around a drift of paper littering his desk again, pushing some off the edge, and onto a similarly littered floor, checked the angle of his bow-tie and scratched a pink and balding dome.

"Ah! On my head all the time!" he said to himself, lowering a pair of half-moons onto his nose. "Must find all these blasted applications."

He got up and traipsed round the office, treading carefully to avoid dusty piles of papers, books and magazines. The room was a crowded mixture of antique furniture, uneasily occupying a space somewhere between the Seventeenth and early Twentieth Centuries. A tall pile of board games – RISK,

Snakes and Ladders, Ludo, Monopoly, 2000 A.D., Dungeons and Dragons – listing precariously from the top of a large oak bookcase further confused the issue.

Presently he came to a standstill back at his desk, picked up and peered at an assortment of papers – here they were – bent down to check the floor nearby, picked up a few more, then sat down ready to sift them through. Carefully he reached inside his waistcoat, and extracted an antique ivory snuff box, placed it on the desk and eased it open. Right hand picked up two small pinches of dark snuff speckled with a white powder and deposited them on left. Quickly, he took in two snorts, then raised his head, sniffing, dabbing nose with 'kerchief.

The first application seemed to be from someone with a blue pen and a penchant for joined-up writing; the second from a person perhaps interested in Bonsai tree cultivation and diminutive notepaper manufacture. Into the grate they flew. This third looked more promising. Typed on a Remington model 32 if he wasn't mistaken.

Erich scanned the pages and wrote a name down on a fresh sheet of Evans pharmaceutical jotter. Above, he titled 'shortlist', using a tacky Taiwanese digital pen.

*   *   *

Jane swept downstairs, narrowly avoided a confrontation with Carol's mountain bike and tried to get her jacket zip up; she stepped forward and noticed a pile of envelopes. She was late; picked them up and flicked through, one for her. She put the others on the meter box, opened the door, slit hers open and stepped out, slamming it behind her. Making for the front gate she pulled the contents out. It was from Brookview Hospital.

Dear Ms. Ashley,

        Thank you for your recent application for employment. I would be pleased to interview you within the next 10 days. Please telephone my receptionist for an appointment.

        Yours sincerely,

        Prof. E. Heisenberg

She re-read the invitation and turned around, straight back to her phone. The call was successful, confirming an appointment for that very afternoon. Next she phoned work, professing dizzy spells. The morning was spent at Hair Butts and frantically swotting up R.D. Laing's *Man, Mind and Madness.*

     *   *   *

Sat worrying in the waiting room, Jane was about as prepared as anyone got for meeting the Professor. An elderly lady she recognised from the morning's phone conversation introduced herself as Miss Dwight, periodically plying her with tea as she assimilated the contents of Punch magazine (Doctor's edition – Not to be read by Patients) '86-90.

Occasionally she could hear voices, and a television set blaring, several rooms away. Was this a psychological test to keep her waiting so long, she wondered, glancing at her watch.

Beside the sofa she occupied was a small occasional table supporting a simple wooden solitaire set. Did she really want to work here? Had she made a mistake to come at all? Perhaps Dave could give her a job in his burgeoning emporium. Again she went to the toilet. Unfortunately this was reached directly from the waiting room, giving no opportunity to investigate or explore.

Back on the sofa she gave the solitaire set another examination, and picked out the central peg. This was the way it went. Rotationally symmetrical, peg over peg, like an amputee snowflake, dancing, disintegrating. Triumphantly she removed the final one, leaving a single projection from the board's centre, proud to recollect moves she hadn't performed since childhood.

Miss Dwight reappeared.

"Would you like to come through now? I'll put the pieces back."

Jane gave her an alarmed look, and followed down a dark panelled corridor. Miss Dwight knocked on the Professor's door and led Jane into an unbelievably cluttered room. He stood up and shook her hand.

"Jane Ashley. Two hours forty five minutes," said Miss Dwight, leaving immediately.

"Ah! Hello, Miss Ashley. Sorry to keep you waiting so long." He was obviously not. "Please have a seat."

She drew one up and sat down, looking around. "Pleased to meet you, D, Professor Heisenberg."

"Right, now what on Earth makes you want to work with mentally ill patients?"

Jane started. "Well – I don't, particularly. I'd be happier if we lived in a society which didn't produce such rampant distress. I do try to make the world a better place though, and I like to help people however I can. I'm qualified, and experienced and willing."

"Well," said the Professor "that seems as good an answer as any." He picked her application up and scanned through it.

The applicant seemed to know what she was about. She was pleasant, and had an impressive work record for one so young, with fair enough sorts of hobbies and interests. She had put 'Hobbies' on her CV, although no woman of his acquaintance had ever actually had a hobby as such. At least not an obsession, which is what most reasonable men took the word to mean.

He edged another look at her over the form. She was quite attractive; medium height and build, good legs protruding from her black, knee length skirt, smallish breasts; light brown hair and blue eyes adorning a sweet and honest face. Yes, the patients would like her.

"You've worked around the country a bit."

"I did some placements from college" explained Jane. "and some voluntary work for the Schizophrenia Trust two years ago."

"Yes, very good. How did you find it?"

"Rewarding, fulfilling. Very hard work."

They discussed Jane for a while longer, then the subject turned to Brookview and the Professor.

"I have my own theories on treatment of mental illness" began Heisenberg. You can study them in some depth later. My great uncle was the famous physicist Werner Heisenberg. Here are some of my books. I do of course draw exhaustively from Leary, Laing, Jung *et al*. Are you familiar...?"

"Oh yes" nodded Jane, "a little." He continued.

"To rebuild the shattered psyche, we must provide warmth, friendship, stability, outlets for creativity", he gestured expansively, getting into his stride. "Brookview is a place where these needs are met, where patients can find meaning in their lives and gather some self-respect. I try to make the atmosphere as much like a family as possible." Jane nodded with him, wishing that she had not had quite so many cups of tea.

"The lynch-pin of successful treatment being...", he raised an eyebrow "...rules and routine."

Three large guardians of time, one a grandfather, filled the silence with a syncopated triplet of ticks.

Heisenberg clamped his hands together. "In order for informality to predominate the general life of our patients, most rules are restricted to board games. As the players learn one set of rules, we give them another, steadily more complex as they progress. From Ludo to role-playing fantasy. By learning to obey rules and play games proficiently, they also learn how to survive Twentieth Century society. Could you be a Gamemaster, a referee, a playleader?"

"Yes," spoke Jane.

"Have you ever played a fantasy or role-playing game?"

"On my brother's computer, yes," she said.

"And when could you start?"

"First of May.

"Right then, I'll let you know in a few days. Miss Dwight'll show you round." He hit a brass bell on his desk.

Miss Dwight re-appeared and duly obliged.

*   *   *

Jane stepped outside, scrunched her eyes and stretched; made straight for Pete's. Weird place, very comfortable, funny staff, strange patients.

The curtain moved a moment after her pebble hit the window. Debbie waved and came down to open the door. Jane shut it, eased past a collection of huge speaker cabinets and passed the front room – full, as always, of variously disembowled motorbikes.

"How 'y' doin' ?" they asked each other.

"Fine."

"I think I've just landed a new job," added Jane, treading on an alsatian's paw in the darkness. He yelped and ran up the stairs before them. "Oh dear."

Debbie pushed the flat's doors and they arranged themselves inside, amongst the sofas and rugs. Ripple bounded over and tried to lick Jane's face off but she pushed the bitch back, stroking her from a distance.

"I can't understand why it didn't record", Lisa was saying.

"Hello Pete," said Jane.

"I know the levels were set right because Flying Teapot came out cracker."

"Hi Jane," he replied. "How're things?"

"Oh sound."

"Was the tab pushed out?" asked Jo.

"I've just been for a job interview. Thanks." She pulled hard on the joint. Debbie passed a hashtray.

"Where?"

"On the second track. It just cuts off."

"Got a light?"

"At a private mental home. By the river."

"Use a candle. It gets you more stoned."

44

"Do they let you out at weekends?"

"I think so..."

"Well, did the button go down?"

Jane lay enraptured by the wood fire and looked up at Pete's dangling cycle frames. The wheels were suspended by hooks, flying over fields of cacti on a fluorescent fish tank in the bay window.

"If I get it, I'll throw a party," she announced.

"Get what?" asked Lisa.

"This job in the hospital. D'you want to come?"

"When?"

"Two weeks next Saturday."

"Yeah."

And so it was settled. Jane received the job offer ten days later and wrote back saying that she would be delighted to accept. She handed in her notice to the City's social services. The party loomed.

5 INFO KNOT

"Ah, Rob. Could I see you later this morning? Ten perhaps? In my office. Good, good. Project review. See how things are going."

"Ten, then. See you then." Robert nodded. And he had thought it was merely not going to be a good day. He could see it looming up like that poster of a granite 'Monday' word, crushing that cretin of a cat, Garfield. Not that it was Monday. No, it was Wednesday, and he had spent the entire previous evening drinking with empty-headed Josella. He'd probably have a finished waveform modelling routine to show Colin if it hadn't have been for her. Now he was going to have to spend all morning explaining infant school calculus to a man with the attention span of a gnat, and intellect to match.

How annoyingly inefficient it is having to talk to people, he thought. Makes you wonder why we installed such an astonishingly expensive computer network system.

Colin sidled into his office. Now, what did the day hold? Problems, decisions, lunch. He cast an appreciative eye over the primed coffee machine (what *would* he do without Josella?) and lounged back in his lovely leather swivel chair. It was one of those you can spin round in, then retract your legs and go even faster. Connolly hide, German bearings: just like his car.

He paged Josella: "FT please Jo, appointments and a coffee, not necessarily in that order", smiling at his little joke. She arrived almost as his finger left the phone.

"Here you are, Colin. Mr Jenkins at eleven thirty. A John Garrick from Techknowledge phoned trying to sell you something, and the project review meeting's been put off 'til Monday."

"Excellent!" he beamed. "Get back to Mr Garrick, tell him I'll see him at twelve thirty. And I'm seeing Robert at ten."

Back at his desk, Robert typed his access code into the terminal, logging on with satisfaction. He made a directory listing of current files, then sat back, thinking. Communications ... yes, the post. He opened his briefcase and withdrew a handful of envelopes. He opened them all, threw away the envelopes and studied the contents. He threw away half the contents too, then noted bills from the credit card and telephone companies and moved his lips, reading a letter from his building society. '... in line with The Bank of England and other lending institutions ... has been necessary to increase additional ... per calendar month...' He boiled inwardly. Why didn't they just put him in chains and have done with it. Now he probably wouldn't be able to go to Egypt for Christmas. Damn them!

Filing the junk back in his briefcase he turned back to work, finding it hard to concentrate. He made new printouts and assigned old ones to the shredding pile, then sat nursing a coffee, thinking of what to say to Colin.

Presently he rose and walked into the boss's office. Colin was reading through a sheaf of papers and motioned for him to sit. A minute later he put them down.

"Hello Rob. How are things going with Stealthcomms?"

"I think they're going very well," began Robert. "With the proviso that this *is* original research in a completely new field. What we've done so far would certainly justify a paper or two in the academic world." Colin nodded. "We've been through a lot of the leading theories in basic electromagnetic wave analysis. This program", he dumped a hefty printout on the imposing pine desk, "accurately models sub-electronic particle behaviour in the real world. We're now working on expansions of it, to predict how light and radio would behave in lower dimension universes – Flatworld and Lineworld we call them."

Colin seemed to smile and frown at the same time in a way only he knew how to do. "The problem is that this isn't academia. This is an engineering company. The Ministry is underwriting our research but they do expect product at the end of the day. How long do you expect this phase of the project to take?"

Robert shrugged. "Six months?"

"And beyond that, what?"

"Beyond that it gets highly speculative. The wave's behaviour has to be extrapolated to five or six dimensions. Then we find a way of suppressing its 'visible' components, reconstructing them from sidebands at the receiver. I'd certainly find a particle accelerator very useful."

"And very expensive. Have you costed it?"

"CERN in Switzerland is available at short notice for special military applications. No more than three or four hundred thousand pounds."

Colin let the tension tighten as he lit a small cigar. "Do you need it?"

"I'm not sure," replied Robert honestly.

"The board won't like it. I'm not sure if I do, and I have to like it first. Can you give me a report to mull over by the weekend?"

"You'll have it by Friday," promised Robert. Colin rose and turned to stare out of the window. "Include a section on repercussions of a fifty percent budget cut. The project review meeting's been put off to Monday afternoon. I may need you to be there. Right well, better get started. See you later." Robert rose and withdrew. Colin continued to contemplate an ornamental fountain within the building's inner quadrangle.

Returning to his terminal, Robert made a few notes about the meeting in his 'to do – current' file. He locked the file and went over to see Phil, speaking in a practised sing-song Swedish accent. "Halo. I'd lik to buy som de-odourant pleas".

Phil replied in a similar vein. "Cerrtainly sirr. Bal orr arrasol."

"No. I want it furr my arrampits." finished Robert. Pleasantries over he spoke again. "So, how's it going, Phil?"

"Oh, not too bad, Rob. I've just squashed this doughnut into flatworld. Now it's got two edges."

Phil moved a mouse he held in his right hand on the desk and clicked its nose. A cross-sight on the screen stopped moving and, after a moment, disappeared. The doughnut started to inflate, showing granules of white sugar glistening on its reddish brown surface. When it reached a plump roundness the squiggles became apparent. They were Egyptian hieroglyphics.

"Hmm." Robert peered at the object. "What are the squiggley lines on it for?"

"Got them off the B-52's album cover," explained Phil proudly. "Digitised the bastards."

"Nice one," agreed Robert. "Er, Colin's just asked me to do a report for Friday. Could I pass on the interrupt? Wavemod needs some plausibility tests doing."

"Sure."

"I'll squirt through a seven day copy with the procedures."

This was common practice. All programs and data within the computer system were coded with possessor's name, and expiry date if on loan. Another hidden file associated with Wavemod would register the creation and destination of every copy. The information liked this. It travelled where it was needed, and felt snug and warm and safe within the Fujisu's tall, grey padded walls. Superfluous editions erased themselves when their time came, while pirated ones could at any time corrupt randomly chosen files, from the unfortunate bootlegger's memory sector. The virus responsible was insensitively and predictably named AIDS.

"How's it going at your end? Finished anything yet?"

"Finished...? This job? It's bloody beginningless."

The pair decided to go for lunch later at the firm's subsidised restaurant. This was located on another site, five minutes drive away.

Robert placed his tray down on an isolated table away from the window, closely followed by Phil. They sat, stacked their trays and began to eat.

"What would they do with this if we ever managed to make it?" wondered Phil.

"Give all civil servants an untraceable hand-held radion't."

"Radion't?"

"This radio doesn't, or won't. No traceable signal," explained Robert, smirking. "It isn't a radio." He glanced around. "An instant secure communications network, or – *chain of command.*"

"To what range do you think?" asked Phil.

"Well as the waves'd be in five or six - D, they wouldn't have any problems going round corners. World-wide coverage for a hundred milliwatts probably."

"That would make someone very powerful," said Phil quietly.

"With a correctly coded access structure, you'd have a very efficient pyramid. The opposition wouldn't like it."

"Very sexy," agreed Phil. "Information..."

They stacked their plates and got up.

"...Is power" finished Robert, locked into a stare with his colleague.

*   *   *

Back home at last, Robert unloaded his carrier bags from the supermarket and threw them away. He hung his jacket up in the hall, took out a thick black wallet and contemplated it carefully before placing it down on a table in the living room. Filling the car with petrol had just cost an extra fiver compared with a few weeks ago. And who got that? he wondered rhetorically. Dirty stinking Arabs with their fingers round the world's neck; nomads and camel-herders a generation back.

He poured himself a larger-than-usual whiskey and put his feet up on the sofa. They could go to Hell if they thought they were getting their hands on his work. Look at the arms Argentina and Iraq had bought from the West. Allies one minute, enemies the next.

He pressed a button on the remote control by his side and suppressed a feeling of nausea as the Prime Minister's face appeared on the Sony's screen, flicked through the other channels then switched it off.

What if he brought the project home? He could get on with it in peace, give it his full attention, keep it safe. Why not? Security at work. Even he would have difficulty smuggling the data out, what with random bag searches and phone recordings. The consequences of discovery would be grave.

Really he needed to do it through an invisible radio data link.

<u>6</u>   AT PLAY

Suddenly the party stopped looming and happened. The flat seemed to be ready around mid-morning, then Emma and Jake called round about one for some tea and cheese on toast. Jane put on an Augustus Pablo dub tape and Jake got his game of RISK out of a large black carrier bag – Matta's International Foods. He had been promising to bring it for a few weeks, and now seemed an opportune time to get back into it.

"This new version isn't as good as the old one," he explained. You used to have to put two boards together and it went on for days."

"Anyone got any cardboard?" asked Emma.

Rain slashed the windows intermittently. It seemed an auspiciously nasty day out for staying inside and being cosy in front of the fire with a few friends. Jane got the toast together and Emma finished rolling her joint.

"I'll be blue," announced Jane.

"Right, count thirty armies. The triangles are five and the squares ten." Jake dealt the cards. They placed armies according to their cards on a board-map of the World, then amassed battalions to fight for continents. Emma started her go by taking four extra armies and annihilating Jake's red forces in Australasia by a lucky turn of the dice.

Jane was next, attempting to consolidate her position in the Americas.

Jake fought back, taking most of Africa. The tiny world sat on its coffee table colourfully, focal point of the room.

Halfway through the game, the doorbell rang. It was a soaked and bedraggled Rick. He followed Jane in and took his coat off.

"Wow! It's really cold out there. Got any tea?"

"In the pot," said Jake pointing. Rick helped himself to a mug and asked who was playing blue, dominating the left hand side of the board.

"Me!" said Jane, spraying him with the fizz from a newly opened can of lager.

"What cards have you got?" he asked, sneaking a look at their small empires of cannons, infantry and cavalry. He gave a conspirital nod, then removed a tin box decorated with mushrooms and 'Om' signs from his jacket pocket.

"Got any acid?" asked Emma, getting straight to the point.

"Purple mikes, Turtles, Windowpane," answered Rick.

"What're the Purple mikes like?" asked Jane.

"Very strong. Rushy. Three fifty."

"I'll have one" she said.

He picked out a tiny purple microdot pill and handed it to her as she passed him the change. She put it on her tongue, swallowed and washed it down with a swig of lager. Stoned as she was, Jane thought she could feel an immediate tingle run down her legs. The others were buying some too. Her eyes were fixed on the board. Blue needed to push into Europe and Asia, consolidating North and South America. She could cash in three infantry cards soon for ten men.

They returned to the game, spellbound. Rick skinned up another joint, and switched on the television without sound. He delved in his coat for a video cassette. Jake eventually managed to break Emma's South-Eastern stronghold; two moves later she was eliminated, and volunteered to go for pizza. Jane changed the tape to some funky jazz. Red and Blue fought a few mighty battles, then Blue gained the upper hand and forced Red to surrender.

"Loser puts it away," said Jane.

"Looks better if I mix the colours up in the boxes like this," said Jake.

"Can I put this Led Zeppelin on?" asked Rick

"Sure," they murmured.

Jane's television had a loose speaker which always resonated on certain notes of music and speech.

The doorbell rang, making Jake jump. It was Dave.

"Oh Hi. Nice Party," he said looking around.

"It's not really started yet," said Jane. "Except for the World Domination preliminaries. Have some pizza." She laughed.

"Emma's not back yet." said Jake. The doorbell rang.

After some fussing about with plates, knives and drinks they all settled down in front of 'The Song Remains the Same'.

"Best rock film of all time," said Rick. Jane was certainly enjoying it so far. Dave opened his organic wine and explained that he hadn't shut the shop early – it was already seven o'clock. Jane started to wander in her mind weather it was a faulty speaker or her ear making the distortion. Whatever it was, it was adding something beautiful to the performance. Impossibly fast lead guitar writhed around a lean, tight and heavy bass and drum sound. Gangsters, streams and hills switched to backstage in New York, frontstage, then a moody gothic fantasy, motorbike scene and wizard with technicolor sword. She was mesmerised with sensation. It seemed to have been going on for ever. One long riff of delicate rhythms and melodies filling the ether. Made for asid.

Parties can generally be said to have *episodes* during which *different things happen* or the participants happen to be in *different states of mind*. The episodes are sometimes clear-cut, such as when the music or lighting changes, sometimes gradual, as when a great many people arrive at different times, and are sometimes purely subjective.

By the time the film ended, there were too many people to watch TV and someone put a fast dance tape on. People swayed, raved and talked. Jane took Dave's head in her hands and told him that he was beautiful, and that she loved him. Debbie came over and asked about the new job.

"Oh I can't believe it!" said Jane "I'm starting a new job and falling in love and earning lots more money. All my friends are here. I'm so in love and so happy.

"You're very lucky" said Jan. "I'm very happy for you. It couldn't be happening to a nicer person."

Things quietened down around three or four; eventually the last revellers left. Jane pulled Dave's head into her lap and held him close. "Let's go to bed".

*   *   *

"Shit! It's nearly eight." Dave kissed Jane and bounded out of bed, hopping into his trousers.

"What, where, huh, what'cha doing, Dave?" asked Jane sleepily. "Come back. It's Sunday.

"I've got a paper round to do." he explained, back to her, pulling on a shirt.

"A what? How old are you?"

"Thirty. You know the store's not doing very well at the moment. I have to make ends meet somehow."

"Oh Dave, there must be other ways. Move in with me. Come back to bed."

"Sorry Jane, I've got to go."

"Oh Da–ave," she whined, getting up and pressing her warm body against him.

"I'll come back when I've finished and make breakfast."

"OK," she murmured. "But I'll make it for you. Hold on. I'll see you out." She slipped on a red dressing gown and led the way through the dead party and downstairs to the front door. They kissed again, wetly, and he stroked her breast through the material.

"Jane, I think I do love you."

"Come back soon!" she replied, and pulled the door open.

They gasped, and Jane was suddenly aware that she was still tripping. Icy snow lay everywhere. Early sunlight sparkled and shone. She closed the door. They stood for a long deep breath.

"Can it be?"

"It can."

Again they kissed. She opened the door again and this time let him go, watching, drinking in the scene through the eyes of a child.

7   WORRYING GAMES

Is worry an altered state of consciousness? In Dave's case it was not. It was his normal, everyday mode of thinking, and he always made sure that he had a stash of freshly depressing literature available to while away worryingly long periods of inactivity behind the Health Store's counter, to remind and inform him of the World's imminent ecollapse.

Of course, being in love did interfere with his worrying somewhat, but then on the other hand it did raise quite a few more problems to nag at him from time to time, too. Now that things had been carnally consummated, as it were, there was always the possibility of a wilfully errant sperm making a rendezvous with one of Jane's presumably free range eggs, for example.

He frowned at a fund-raising letter from the Party and regretfully filed it in the paper-recycling bin.

What could a gorgeous nymphet like Jane possibly see in him? She had the World an oyster at her feet. Not that she ate oysters. Neither of them did. They had interests in common perhaps, he supposed, and a sort of chemistry between them not entirely composed of hallucinogens. If only she wouldn't insist on playing games all the time, and making him join in. The last few times he'd called round, Mo had been there with various permutations of Jake, Emma, Steve and Rick, throwing strangely improbable dice.

A customer entered and bought a packet of red lentils. Dave made a note in his stock control book. That was the second one this morning. Not bad. At this rate he'd soon be able to give up the paper round.

Yes, he could see a new Jane blossoming over the past few weeks. She was loving it at the hospital. He cracked up at some of her funny stories. Were some of them a betrayal of professional confidence? Probably. And would he ever get off as a plastic goblin in a fantasy world printed on cardboard? Probably not. He looked through to the phone in the back room and idly contemplated calling her, to make sure she was still there.

A mile or two away, Jane pottered about in the Staff Office. She felt comfortably secure amongst the patients' files, the drugs cabinet, rotas, reports and game charts. Natch, not too much of this boring stuff to do before gametime. She had to admit it: there was a very competitive urge in her, she needed to win, even against opponents with the most unfair handicap. Should she take one out and see who wanted to play? Or gather a team together and pick something they all liked? Oh just go and do it, she thought. She left the office, locked it and went through into the living room.

Heidi had her tongue out, her best blank expression on, and was moaning softly as she rocked back and forth in her chair.

Frank had a finger in his mouth and was shuffling back and forth, taking an onslaught of verbal abuse from Malcolm.

Liz sat with her legs apart, knobbly knees poking out of a denim skirt, a finger digging her nose. She was watching television intently.

"What's the point?!" shouted Malcolm. "I can't see the telly! You're so su, su, so, su su, sit down!" He noticed Jane and became all charm. "Ah hello. Tell Frank, will you? I can't see the telly."

"Sit down, will you, Frank" she said. He shuffled off into a corner and sat, looking up with surprised eyes. "What's on, Liz?" No reply. Jane moved between her and the TV. "What's on?" Liz stirred, and tried to see past Jane's commanding figure.

"It's a quiz," she ventured. "And I can't see. And Malcolm's shouting"

"I am not!" he shouted, with all the force of a heavyweight tenor.

"Come on guys," said Jane. "Let's play something." She turned round and snapped the TV off.

It was a nice clear moment. The hearty applause and questions, the beepers and buzzers and gongs vanished. One's heartbeat slowed. What a splendid room. Someone had gone to all the trouble of picking out ceiling mouldings in a different colour paint, purple, red and blue on white. The wallpaper was a gentle fawn, with a modern sort of block design pattern in repeats. The armchairs and sofa, a brushed electric blue, sat on lush carpet of a darker hue.

"What's it to be, then?"

"I want to play Batman" said Malcolm.

"Who wants to be Robin?" asked Jane rhetorically. Nobody else ever wanted to play this non-existent game, and this was the etiquette for turning him down.

"Quiz!" said Liz

Jane looked out of the window and turned her eyes

skywards to the chemical smog over the Mersey. *Trivial Pursuit* had not really been a success story here. Indeed, she had been the only player to answer a question correctly.

"How about *Sorry*?" she suggested.

"I always like a quiz." said Malcolm. "It's my greatest joy. Ask me anything, anything at all. Come on now, don't be shy. Who won the F.A. Cup in 1973? hm? Sunderland. Eleven-nil."

"Quiz!" said Liz.

"Just a minute," said Jane. "I'll see what there is." She walked out to see the Professor, down the dark and now familiar corridor, knocked and entered.

"Ah, hello Jane", he looked up, brightly.

"Professor, do you have any simple quiz games please? I tried *Trivial Pursuit* but that was too hard."

He pursed his lips. "Have you tried a bit of research? *The Times*, *Sports Yearbook*, that sort of thing?"

"For the patients."

"Ah yes, the patients. Tell me..."

She waited. "Tell you what?"

"Tell me. It's a simple quiz. Let me find it."

It was a constant source of amazement to Jane how Heisenberg could find anything in here. 'A psychiatrist could have a field day with this man,' she thought.

He flicked through the oak bookcase, head bent, and picked out a small box.

"Here it is" he said triumphantly, placing it before her. "Finest therapeutic tool this side of Pluto." He opened the box and removed a set of cards, a small metal spinning wheel. "Tell me..." he started. "A book beginning with..." – the wheel span – "G."

"Gone with the Wind," she answered.

"That's a film isn't it?" he asked.

"It was a book first."

"Very well. Jane Ashley *un point*."

"Ideal. Thanks Prof."

She packed it back up and returned to the living room.

"I've got it!" she exclaimed, taking the wheel out and placing it on the floor. "All sit down, then we can start. Come on Heidi, Frank." With something more than a bit of persuasion they were finally encouraged to gather round. Jane took a notebook and pen out of her top pocket and drew five initials, five columns. "You'll pick it up really easily; let me answer the first question or two then we'll start properly." She picked a card out and span the wheel. Frank, Liz and Malcolm gazed apprehensively. "A mountain beginning with ...W." No one said anything for a while. "Oh well, maybe there isn't one. I'll spin again."

"Watzman!" Liz ejaculated.

"Watzwhat?" Eventually she said it again.

"Watzman."

*   *   *

Back in the Health Store, Dave picked up the phone and began to dial, for it was five past one. Frosty Dwight answered, and reluctantly put him through to Jane.

"Yeah, Dave I'm blooming ... Well ... fourteen hours ha ha ... Just in the middle of a quiz ... Only *three*! Listen, d'you know of any Watzman mountains? ... Never mind about the correct political projection of the thing, just look in the index ... That's great, absolutely brilliant, I knew you had a use somehow ... What? ... Yeah tonight ... Love you too, baby ... Bye."

Liz got one for that. Plus a bonus point for being extra smart. Had she ever been to Innsbruck?

"A colour beginning with... B – Frank!"

"B," He chewed a fingernail and frowned. "B," he repeated, unsure. "Yellow?"

"No" she said miserably. "Heidi?"

"Mgrrughghghghar," came the reply. That was good. It was a response.

"Black!" said Malcolm. Jane knew that technically black is not a colour, rather the absence of it of any kind, but gave it him anyway.

"A city beginning with ... V ?"

"Venice!"

"An animal beginning with ... R ?

"Rabbit!"

This was really working well.

"An illness beginning with ... I ?"

*   *   *

"Do you want to go for a drink?"

asked Jane at Debbie's doorway.

"All right". She could do with one, and by the look of things so could Jane. "I'll just get my coat."

Jane waited in the gloomy hallway a while, then Debbie clip-clopped back down and they were out. It was eight, fairly light but cool. The bar was still fairly empty. Jane sat down at their corner table with a glass of house red. "How have you been keeping?" she asked.

"OK, OK really," said Debbie, raising her full glass. "Cheers."

"Going anywhere this year?"

"Maybe France."

"With Pete?"

"Mmm. What about you?"

"And Dave? Haven't really discussed it yet. Suppose he'd have to close the shop."

"Would you like to?"

"Yeah. We remain besotted. A holiday would be nice. I still don't think I know him all that well yet. He's very quiet and self-contained, "

"Not like Pete," laughed Debbie interrupting.

"so we just need some space together alone, I think," finished Jane. They sipped in silence for a bit, listening to shreds of conversation from other tables. "Men usually are distant, anyway. It can take a lot to get them to open up."

"Trust" said Debbie, "and time."

"And not too many people. He isn't assertive enough in groups. His thoughts come slowly and delicately, like butterflies." Her attention wandered back to Debbie from a picture on the wall she had been studying.

"I think Pete's are like Pigeons." Jane returned to her contemplation of the picture.

"I suppose we could get a week off."

"So they do let you out at weekends." They smiled.

"Occasionally."

"Settled in yet?"

"I think there's a limit to how settled in I want to feel. It's all very strange, except for Mary and Margaret. They're doing similar sort of work to me. Married. Square. Don't see a lot of them. The Professor's very eccentric. Typical I suppose, and then there's Miss Dwight, his hench-woman. Yes, I'm getting to know them."

"What about the patients?"

"Hmm. Mostly all right. Like children really, funny children. Not as bad as Emlyn's brats."

8   FRACTAL TRANSMISSIONS

Robert guided the obtrusively loud mower up and down his garden. It was funny how he put the chore off so much, because once started it did relax him; he enjoyed doing the lawn immensely. At the end of every stripe the motor died to silence and he would turn, pick up the electric cord, and with a flick of his wrist, wave it out of the way.

The garden reflected his attitude to housework in general. He kept it fairly tidy. He didn't invite anyone else to come and mess it up. It was a functional, low maintenance piece of liveware with recreative potential. Various inherited bushes and plants struggled to grow around the lawn's border. Robert considered weeds an essential part of a flourishing vegetative microsystem, thus excusing himself the further chore of identifying and pulling them out, at least, perhaps, until he had a machine to help him in the task. There was a brief area of paving between house and lawn. He had brushed this before plugging in the mower. At the bottom of the garden there stood a wooden shed on the right, a shouting mass of floribunda on the left. Robert's elderly neighbours the Smiths, whose semi-detached house adjoined his, had for some time been expressing unwarranted concern about its size, and presumed potential for further growth.

Robert stopped at the end of another row and willed evil thoughts towards their blossoming apple tree. He bent down again and twirled the cord out of the way. Cordless lawnmowers. That would be a nice harmless radion't spin-off. He gripped the handle again and screamed another flurry of grass out of the mower's jaws. He had his scruffy faded jeans on with wasted trainers. An old Greek printed T-shirt rippled gently on his lean torso, blown by the early evening breeze.

He looked back at his work and went to unplug the mower. Sometime from within his subconscious mind a train of thought began to take shape. He looped the cord round his lower arm. There was a small chance this stealth communications might prove elegantly simple. He leaned the mower on its side and went into the shed to get the filthy old towel he used to clean its blades. He could set up an experiment. On the UHF television waveband. Try out a five-D antenna, a fractaerial. Use Wavemod as test data. Transmit anything really. In code.

Lovingly he wiped the grass and mud from the long curved blades. His video recorder could be left on the timer to capture transmission.

Standing on tip-toes, Mrs Smith watched Robert over the net curtain in her back bedroom. She lowered herself, tutted, and gingerly trod her way out of the room and down to the lounge. Her husband was quietly relaxing in front of the television with a crossword.

"Poor man. Always moping about. He needs a good woman to get him out of himself."

"Mr Ashley?"

"Yes. It seems such a pity. A nice young man like him going to waste."

Mr Smith reached into a pocket of his cardigan for a rubber and erased a word.

"Of wisdom. Ten letters. S something P something something something something something A something."

"I'm sorry. I just don't know, dear. Would you like a cup of tea?"

"Mmm..."

While Mrs Smith pottered in her kitchen, Robert was now plotting in his den. For a home laboratory it was lavishly equipped, with enough processing power to satisfy the requirements of a small régime's secret police force. He would need some extra equipment for this, though. Quickly he scribbled a list then went back down it, pointing with pencil, ticking. He took some catalogues from a shelf above the workbench and flicked through, marking pages, stood up and left.

Mrs Smith answered the two chimes of her doorbell promptly. She looked very slightly unnerved, guilty he thought.

"Oh hello, Robert, how are you?"

"Fine," he replied. "How are you?"

"Very well, thanks. Would you like to come in?"

"Thanks, but I can't just now. I was just wondering if you could take in a few parcels for me over the next few days."

"Arriving in the morning?"

"Yes, they should be."

"No trouble at all. It's difficult when you're out at work, isn't it?" she pried. Robert agreed and politely took his leave.

The next day he placed orders, and spent his evenings that week unpacking, testing and setting up the instruments. With the aid of one he tuned an unused channel of the video recorder to an exact frequency; another box contained the interface needed to use it as a data recorder with the computer.

Saturday morning brought the arrival of television aerial engineers. After explaining his interest in Irish and continental programmes, he had some difficulty refusing their hard sell of a satellite receiver dish.

At work he was obtaining similar, compatible equipment, and had designed a suitable transmitter fractaerial on his workstation. The mechanical engineering department in Essex would have it built up and delivered in a few days.

It was all the lab waited for. Robert had been playing cards very close to his chest. He explained the experiment as vague tests, preliminary work. He had given the project planning meeting just enough hope to keep his funding secure.

This was a small room, not unlike his lab at home. Similarities included two identical Olivetti microcomputers, poised, primed to exchange a very special stream of data.

Robert took a lead from the nineteen inch rack's 'scope and twisted it onto a spare spectrum analyser input. He frowned intently and twisted a few controls, turned fast at a knock on the door.

Josella entered confidently in her smart red suit and high heels. "*Good morning* Robert, and how are you today?"

"Wonderful, Jo." he replied. "Nearly as good as you look."

"There's another parcel for you at reception. Bloody enormous. I hope you don't blow us all up." She looked at him quizzically, the sides of her pouting red lips curling into the semblance of a smile.

"Well, if that's what I think it is, the messenger deserves a reward. How about lunch? I could kilobyte to eat."

"You're stopping for *lunch*? With a new toy just arrived? That's not like you at all, Robert." He returned her catty look.

"I may get deeply engrossed with this baby, and I don't want to be interrupted by tea."

"Wavers?"

"Right you are."

She left. He followed for his parcel. It was big, but not heavy, attracting a series of impertinent suggestions from more cretinous occupants of the airy software development suite he took it through.

With reverence he placed it on the lab's floor, took a knife and slit the seal. He bent the cardboard back, took out the top polystyrene packing piece and reached inside. Here was a silver chandelier the Sultan of Brunai would kill for, he thought, placing it on a purposefully clear area of the workbench.

The device gleamed with precision. In a way, it reminded him of the Catholic Cathedral on Hope Street. Tubes and rods flowed into each other flawlessly, like some champion's ruinously expensive cycle frame. He took a micrometer from one of the equipment draws and checked a few dimensions. They were spot on so far as he could measure, which was not all the way. Parts of the structure reproduced themselves in miniature through five recursions, a fractoral pattern. He took a lint-free duster from the same drawer and pointlessly polished one leg.

Licking teeth under pale lips, Robert managed to tear himself away from the creation, bounced into a chair and slid over to the computer terminal. He ran the latest version of Wavemod coupled to his CAD model of the antenna.

The program began in its usual way, displaying a static red dot in the centre of the screen. Robert tapped a key, stepping the simulation up into one dimension. Instantly a blue line appeared over the red dot. It regularly and repeatedly varied in brightness, sliding from one side of the screen to the other. At first it stayed still, then the pattern started to shift, gliding upwards. Perspective shifted, as did the line, panning edges of the screen. It was as if one end of it was stretching miles off into the distance.

He selected 2-D, and a green sine wave appeared over the blue line. It was broad and wavy one end, sharp and compressed at the other, as it too soared and swayed.

His eyes riveted, Robert tapped another key, bringing the simulation into 3-D. Again he saw digital dust, dancing through red, green and blue laser-like sine wave patterns: secret serpents of software. He punched a few buttons on the FM modulator in the rack. The entangled waves continued to be viewed from a variety of angles, still for a moment, then moving again. He licked his lips, then, as he stared, the red wave started flickering, until it barely flashed at all, like a random pitched strobe.

"It's turning" he exclaimed. "Oh God, it's turning. It works."

He managed to get through lunch with Josella somehow, though she did ask why he kept turning his pint glass round and round.

The afternoon flew by. It was seven before all connections had been made to the apparatus. The antenna pointed down a metre-wide tunnel of wave-absorbent panels to a simple indoor TV aerial.

"Tomorrow, my lovely," spoke Robert, leaving for home, where he would work into the early hours.

9   PARKED

The days, nay, the weeks shot past at a rapid pace, until Jane found she had been at Brookview a couple of months, and it was now Midsummer.

Hearty hoards of people lounged outside Keith's Wine Bar and the Albert all through the day, then long, long into the light evening. Young ravers in verted baseball caps patrolled the Lane and park, pedalling mountain bicycles possessing more than a passing resemblance to guillotined day-glo tractors. Huge gnarled trees spread their effulgence wide, in swaying green expanses of vitality, and a hard rhythmic rap attack blended with moody old guitar solos streaming from wide open sash windows. Girl hippies and students were tacitly slaying all males within eyeshot from positions within their sweet summer nothings.

The stench from the pig farm on Little (late *Back*) Parkfield Road was reaching its stinky zenith. Jane wrinkled her nose and moved her head back inside the window. 'Shall I floss my teeth?' she thought, 'or look for something else to iron?' She had a quick think about it over a cigarette while sitting, poised on the edge of a chair. She had been up all night doing the housework; all except the hoovering. That would be better received later.

Absently she took out a tenner from her purse, rolled it up, chopped up, laid out and snorted another line of speed. She decided to start the day's gameplan, and took out the top drawer's contents from a chest by the window.

A few birds chattered outside; the atmosphere was still and calm. Deliberately she placed artefacts on the round glass coffee table:-

Gamemaster's handbook

four 20-sided dice

Character cards

Spell book

Crystal (from *Earthbreeze* in Glastonbury)

Fountain pen

Silverine exercise book

A few pieces of coloured string

The last items were not strictly necessary, but, Jane being the sort of person she was, there they were, should any need arise.

For thirty five minutes she rolled dice, studied the handbook and wrote figures, letters and other symbols down on the pad. She was pleased to finish by rolling a joint of rare sensomelia. Deciding to check out the ducks in Sefton Park, she got outwardly mobile in a matter of mere moments, saving Jay for use as a walking stick.

She couldn't remember feeling this good before, ever. Perhaps it would just go on and on. She closed her mind to the inevitable and dreadful amphetamine hang-over. Energy flooded her mind, body and soul like she was some kind of organic engine with the turbo on full. Forget coke, this was the real thing; two hundred miles into the stratosphere, mind clear, sharp and racing. No holding back, no slowdown, no pain, no uncertainty. Looking down towards the Lane she paused to light Jay, inhaling smoke as clear as mountain air. She could feel it in her nerves, though, almost immediately, tingling, further stimulated. A milk float passed, trundling along; she waved her fingers at the driver and assured him of the goodness of this fine morning.

Running across the road to the park, she jumped the low stone wall and headed for the boating lake. A thousand shades of sunlight shone through the grassy dew. 'I Feel Love!' Jane thought, half regretting not having brought the tape along. She could hear finely detailed sounds of music all around her anyway; ducks barking, distant traffic roaring, birds doing *their* thing, herself and her thudding heartbeat.

She reached a leg up to the wrought iron gate, pulled herself over and onto the island. It was wilder than the rest of the park, solitary, more mysterious, surrounded by a moat that became the lake.

A rabbit rushed past.

Jane decided to sit a while on the bandstand. She crossed her legs, listened and looked around. Feeling secure, content, happy, she took a pack of Rizlas from her shirt pocket and began to roll almost automatically, to reminisce, the same way. The events of the past few weeks were frankly incredible; that she admitted herself. That she alone was knowing and in full control of the information was even more bizarre.

Her thoughts drifted back, overturning. Prediction or control?

*　　　　　*　　　　　*

The patients had been doing well, at least, if measured by their proficiency at game playing. They had really entered into the spirit of it, perhaps too much even, thought Jane, a thought the Professor might have considered blasphemous.

They were deeply involved in another game of RISK: her, Malcolm, Liz and Martin. Martin was a sad casualty of the information age, and, in her judgement, the last man on earth to benefit from game playing 'therapy'. His last job had been writing the things for spotty young males to play on their home computers. Overwork and a growing obsession with the philosophy of Nietzsche and existentialism had taken their toll. 'Raving' would describe him well. Jane stared at him for a moment as he threw his handsome head back, laughing uncontrollably at Liz's loss of Southern Europe. It hadn't been that funny. Not funny at all in fact, unless there was a hidden joke somewhere. She felt a momentary chill shudder through her. It was hard sometimes to be the anchor of sanity, the reference point; the arbiter of sanity.

Malcolm took the red dice, his eyes gleaming, and reached towards the blue army tray. Jane pointed her finger over his territories, counting.

"Just three this time," she said. He appeared to be losing.

"Siberia fights back!" he announced concentrating his forces on one spot of the giant Asian continent, hardest but most precious of all to hold. "Mongolia and all points West."

Martin took a blue defender's die and rolled even before the attack began, smirking while Jane sat, still chilled.

"I am Gorbachev," he said "and my Empire dissolves."

Malcolm, against all laws of probability, had gone on to win Asia and the game.

Later they had all sat watching TV. The news started, and Jane felt the same chill come over her again. Michial Gorbachev's face appeared, followed by a map of the Soviet Union.

"At noon today Armenia passed a law declaring itself autonomous of the Central Soviet Parliament" droned the announcer's voice.

Thoughts inside Jane's head clashed and whirred, like gears trying, failing to engage, cogs biting, seizing, being torn apart.

She had tried to avoid RISK for a while after that, telling herself it was nothing, just coincidence, a chance remark. That night she had gone round to Rick's and become immersed in a sea of hash, Zeppelin, wine, Rush.

They were playing again. Wizards Quest. A simple adventure. Martin's wild enthusiasm had infected everyone. Jane forgot her fears. She was Bison, the boxer. Liz was a tunnel. "I'm a hole between two places" she laughed.

"They shall not pass" murmured Martin (aka The *Rolling Stones* aka the Dragonslayer card) darkly.

They passed from outer to inner worlds. Dragons were indeed slayed. Players played. And died.

Jane couldn't remember who won, didn't want to. The whole day was a haze in her memory, a blur except for that time in the early evening when they were all watching TV again. She was laying knives and forks out on the dining tables. Miss Dwight was prattling on about shift rotas. Liz cried out. Jane's eyes swivelled to her in slow motion, and then the TV. She saw a body being carried, underground. There was a cave. Light strung from the ceiling. The newscaster was saying something about a fatal accident in the Channel Tunnel. A man had been killed while blasting. Her legs turned to jelly. She wanted to go to the toilet, but stayed to listen.

It was a short report, way down just before the sports news. Bison's familiar face stared out at her.

"And in an incident in a New York nightclub, the boxer Dave Bison was arrested and charged with assault after..." Her head swam. Precognition, synchronicity, telepathy??? She thought back to Wizards Quest. What had they done? When?

She excused herself and threw up in the toilet. That had not been the moment she knew. Felt, perhaps, but not knew. 'Why me?' she wondered. Chance? Luck? Karma? It didn't matter.

She didn't know until a few days later. A day of her own, thankfully. A day to let the psyche dissolve, take stock, rebuild itself.

"Three killed in Stones riot," shrieked the headline. Paris. Mayhem. The song 'Sympathy for the Devil'. Gendarmes in a baton charge. Three killed. The words bounced around her head meaninglessly. Memories of Dragons, no, Wizards Quest, did likewise. Why? No, when? Why? How?

*   *   *

But now she smiled. Stubbed a roach on the bandstand's wooden floor. Understood. The Power. The power only she had. The power to *win friends and influence people.*

78

10   SWEAT SUCCESS

Roisín lay beside him as they soaked in the clear Mediterranean sun. They had introduced themselves briefly, made some small talk, then surrendered to the heat and were silent.

She shifted slightly. Robert became aware of her gaze on his lightly tanning torso.

"Do you brown easily?"

"Not like you" he replied. "I've been cooking a week already." She nodded. "Actually I could do with a bit more oil." He reached for the beach bag and removed a bottle of Ambre Solair, protection factor eight. He unscrewed the top and squeezed; a small turd of lotion oozed onto his hand: he began to apply it to his legs.

"Let me do that for you," she suggested, taking the bottle from his hand, and began stroking. The oil lubricated her hands well. He tensed at first, then relaxed as her hot fingers pressed around his neck, down his sides, up, around and round his nipples and chest hair. He looked further away. "It's an empty beach. Why don't we get an all over tan?..."

He blinked. Opener and opener. Shut them again. Tried to go back. Couldn't, then sat up with a start. *Today*, my lovely! Felix yawned and stretched out a razor paw on the sunlit duvet.

Robert threw the cover back and staggered off bathwards. Felix stared at him in disbelief. What made the man so... awake so quickly? He didn't need to be let out yet. The box of noises was silent. Slowly, Felix understood. When you need a wash... He gave his smooth black coat an admiring glance, a perfunctory tonguing, then nestled his smart and lovely head back into white underfur and covered it with his equally magnificent tail.

In his haste, Robert forgot to let the beast out

'so,' thought Felix, finally awakening properly, 'I have the house to myself'. He crunched his way through a hitherto neglected bowl of Kit-e-krunch and lapped a little hairy water from the adjoining receptacle. There was a new table sporting four temptingly smooth legs in the next room, where he could attend to part of his toilet, leaving a few long hints pertaining to breakfast quality and garden access.

After doing this, he jumped up onto the dining room window sill and spent the best part of an hour watching birds, chattering at them and generally letting his hunting instincts give themselves full expression.

The day was pleasantly warm, hot even, but Felix knew all about too much of a good thing and didn't want to waste any of it. When tired of the birds, he ambled out into the living room and found the warmest spot. He circled clockwise a few times, had a short wash, then settled down for his mid-day snooze.

The video recorder slept with him. As Felix's chest rose and fell, the video's digital clock blinked its colon off and on, steadily, relentlessly. At 15:00, it clicked smoothly and began to whirr. Felix, on top, began to purr in sympathy, although he was still asleep.

*   *   *

The figures on his watch blinked, changed over. 15:00. It was time. His fingers flew, entered the command. Down a web of cable the data streamed. To the casual observer nothing was happening. Robert was anything but. His eyes gleamed at the Fujitsu's welcome 'Status OK' report. Outside, up and beyond, uncharted aeons of ether buzzed with an unfamiliar screech. The airwaves were silent; empty.

On the roof of a house a few miles away, pinpointed, charted by high resolution maps, an elaborate television aerial pointed at the lab. The focused signal reappeared in normal space, as standing waves on dipoles. It shot down coaxial cable to a harmless looking video recorder inside the house, finally coming to rest as a pattern of magnetic stripes revolving slowly under a throbbing black and white cat.

Robert flicked up a red toggle switch and closed his briefcase, slamming out of the lab.

"I'm sick," he announced to Josella, striding past her desk.

"You've never looked better" she replied to the swinging doors.

Keep calm, he told himself, it hasn't happened yet. He sat himself inside the car and kept a limpet-like grip on the wheel all the way home. With iron self-control he managed to keep only ten miles an hour above the speed limit. His insides were on fire; he felt the sharp buzz of pure adrenaline. Lots of it.

Home at last. The door thrown shut he stole into the front room, picking up and plonking a surprised and indignant Felix down on the sofa. He unplugged the video recorder and carried it upstairs to the lab. It was quickly reconnected. The Olivetti booted up with a quiet whirr; he pulled the mouse down a menu of options. Run file from archive. Click. And reached a finger forward. *Play.*

WAVEMOD V4.2
WARNING: DISKBOMB IN 30 SECONDS
PLEASE ENTER CODE TO DEACTIVATE

The screen clock began counting down. 30,29,28... So paralysed was he with shock, his fingers punched the wrong code in twice, saving a hundred and twenty megabytes of hard disk with only five seconds to spare. The options page appeared. Slumped back in the chair, he casually reached out and started it; watched the graphics take shape once more, just a model no longer. It hadn't transmitted normally, he knew. The intercept receiver had caught nothing. This was astonishing. Unbelieving, half closing his eyes, he let go his thoughts to run free the instructions and routines known so well.

Time passed. Robert passed, from daze to doze to delirium. There were fish climbing ashore, evolving lungs, vocal chords; the first squawk, or bleat; whatever. Mankind: cavemen, gesturing, grunting; vocalising for the first time. Paper: the first scribe, scratching stick pictures beside the Nile. Gutenberg's printing press, Alexander Bell's telephone, Edison's wax phonograph. Marconi's wireless sparks, Baird's spinning disk television.

Robert Ashley, inventor of the ... the what? Oh well, name it later. Anything but Stealthcomms. Pity he couldn't tell anyone about it.

He got up and ran downstairs. "Felix, Felix, I've just invented the... er... the *Radion't*. Felix was nonplussed. Was it edible? warm? soft? small, furry and animate? He doubted it, and, running to the back door, called for service.

Robert let him out and basked in the glory of the day. *His glory*. Well, he could stay in and gloat some more or have a few beers in the garden to celebrate. Plan his next move. He half-closed his eyes, pursed his lips and slowly nodded, as if the jury's foreman, finally decided on some momentous verdict.

The fridge was dry, so he decided to stroll down to the shops and stock up. He didn't go to the nearest off licence because it enclosed customers in a heavy perspex cage. Robert hated being treated like a criminal. He bought a few four-packs of Stella from the civilised wine vendors up the hill, then headed back for a sunny afternoon of gentle intoxication. The result of his deliberations in the garden was that he should keep 'Radion't' under his hat and see how things went.

The next day, a supposedly recovered but actually slightly hung-over Robert made an early appearance at work. Further intended refinements to Wavemod would gradually render it unusable for any purpose more serious than impressing Josella. He started on that first thing. His attitude of secrecy and slight paranoia went entirely unnoticed; it was normal. No one bothered him too much. Perhaps they thought the phantom sickness was infectious. The only problem he could foresee was that with 'official' research diverted down a stream of red herrings, he would have to do the real development work at home, without the fractaerial. How could he steal such a large object? Getting it out of the front door would be impossible. Really he needed some sort of teleport device.

11   A Secret Shared

"Debbie, I've got to talk to you," pleaded Jane. "Is anyone in?"

"What's up? No, come in." She led the way up to her and Pete's crowded, cosy flat. Jane was stumbling and sniffling behind her.

"There, sit down. Tea?" Jane nodded, Debbie poured.

"Can I talk to you in confidence?" asked Jane. "I've got to tell someone, work it all out into words, but I don't want you to do anything. Just listen." She scrunched her face and bowed her head. Debbie put an arm out round her, and they rocked slowly on the sofa.

"You can tell me" she said, "Of course you can."

"What if anyone comes?"

"I'm out."

"Pete?"

"I'll explain. He can take Ripple round the park again."

Jane's trembling slowly subsided, her breath eased, and she pushed herself to sit a little further back.

"What's it all about? Dave?" Debbie leaned over and flicked off Toxteth Community Radio's gently pulsating vibes.

"No, no, let it come slowly. Games, power, the World. I..." Jane started panting, Debbie comforted her again, and prepared to be patient. A few moments later Jane carried on. "For a start, I know it sounds crazy, so don't call it that or I'll clam up."

"Right."

"It's been like... sort of gradual... an unfolding, or understanding. A slow revelation. You can't lock someone up for knowing something, can you?"

"No," comforted Debbie quietly.

"I thought the World was one thing." She stared into space vacantly. "And then found out it's not. Then I thought I could do something about it, but I don't have any control. I thought I knew, but it's me who's known. I'm like... an instrument of it, without any say. I just don't know what to do." Debbie nursed her through a sudden episode of tears.

"I'm here" she said. "You can cry on me. Just let it all out." Then, though she didn't know why, she was crying too, and they held their arms round each other and kissed their tears. Jane sniffed and wiped a hand on her face.

"We were playing games. I was trying to help them Communicate, think straight. It was going well. Then there was a new patient – Martin. It was gradual, like I said. He said strange things; well, they all did. But he was saying things, like, in the games, then these plays started coming true."

"Like what?"

"Not yet, not now. I can't. It's too painful; deaths; poor, dear people being... manipulated; used?" She frowned at her

86

question. Debbie, puzzled, nodded automatically, in habit and for appearance rather than in any agreement or understanding.

"He's not mad at all. Only with power. I don't know who else is with him. Or how much they know I know. Or what their plans for me are."

"Never mind what you don't know. What do you know for sure?"

"For sure? There's a group. Some of them are pretending to be crazy 'cause it suits their purposes. Some of them may be crazy. They're playing power games behind the scenes. For their own amusement, or maybe... It's like fixing races, but on a much grander scale," she finished lamely.

"It's hard to follow," interjected Debbie.

"Don't I know. They compete against each other. On board games. Only the pieces relate to real people. Politicians, artists, sportsmen, anyone. Through them they can fight real wars, influence billions of people, win bets, make fortunes."

"I see."

"There's so much I don't know. Who they really are? Perhaps I was imagining, guessing, and my thought patterns resonated with what they're doing somehow. Somehow, I was drawn into it. I don't know why or how."

"Do you have proof?"

"I've seen proof with my own eyes, but I can't explain. I can't show it to you, I just need to tell someone, to stay sane."

Debbie's face remained impassive. "Are you still playing?" Jane nodded. "Do you want to stop?"

"Yeah"

"Go on the sick. Leave."

"I can't yet. I'm overdrawn. I can't make them suspicious."

Then she let slip what she hadn't thought she would tell. "I'm in the middle of a long game with some people. I can't say who. My piece relates to someone very close to me, in a way. Something very wonderful could happen, but if I leave, I don't know, they might die. That's all. Don't ask any more."

"Jane, I'm very worried for you." She reached for her hand and held it. "I don't think you know what you..."

"OK, OK," interrupted Jane. "I don't want to know. Thanks for listening. That's all I needed you to do. You've been great. I'll go in a minute. I need to go for a walk by myself."

Resigned, Debbie sighed. "Take it easy Jane. Don't do any more trips. Get out while you're still all right."

"Thanks," said Jane. "It's been hard telling someone. I feel a weight off my mind." She stood up. "Catch you later."

"Anytime," said Debbie, and meant it. Jane left.

Fate had been kind. No one had interrupted them. Now Pete pushed the door open and greeted her with only a few minutes' grace.

"Hi Pete," she said vacantly. "You've just missed Jane."

"Oh, I saw her going out," he replied. "Done any lunch?"

"Mmm". She pondered. "She's in a bad way. I hope it all turns out all right."

"What does? Lunch?"

"Oh nothing. Women's stuff." He turned his gaze up to the window's grimy sky. *Women.*

12   A Secret Kept

For a week or so now, Robert had been furtively testing his invention. A small case of disks in the den bulged with wholesale quantities of classified data and programs filched from work. Measurements had now confirmed and corrected theory. He was pleased with his experiments, and with himself. Thoughts, never still, now turned to further development. What properties did the five-D waves have? And what could be done with them?

Silently he sat at his workstation, and watched Colin wobble back from another business lunch. Pathetic. Ah, but he should be grateful for the man's gullibility. He had a grand appetite for bullshit, to be sure.

"Halo" said Phil.

"Arumpits" replied Robert with a smile.

"What, this?" asked Phil, indicating the screen.

"Too right."

"Solved those Laplace transforms for you." Robert took the printout gratefully. "Fuji's been up all night doing them. Can't see what use they are though."

"None, probably."

"Are we getting anywhere?"

"I'm beginning to doubt it." He clasped palms behind his head and leant back. "A few pretty patterns. Some elegant theoretical ideas." He sighed. "I'm afraid I may have been rather over-optimistic at the project planning meeting. We'll see."

Phil shrugged. "The V-channel MOSFET wasn't built in a day."

"Coffee?" asked Robert. Phil didn't mind if he did, and took a seat while Robert fetched them two black and steaming mugs.

"Any luck with the fractaerial?"

"Nah. Back to the drawing board." He shook his head. "Junk." After a pause he continued. "Actually the transforms are for something else. Another line of enquiry entirely. Information..."

"being what it is." finished Phil.

"I was wondering if Heisenberg's Uncertainty Principle could be applied on a macro scale, quantitatively."

"Really?" quizzed Phil. "I can't see that."

"Take it a step at a time," continued Robert, wagging a finger. "The principle states that we can't know the exact position *and* velocity of a particle at the same time. The observer influences the observed, like a voltmeter taking power from the circuit it's connected to, reducing the measured voltage."

"Or a micrometer, scraping a few atoms off the measured surface," added Phil.

"Precisely. Now, with modern instruments, it's virtually negligible error right down to atomic scale. You can effectively measure the exact position and velocity of a car or a football, no problem."

"But not an electron, or a neutrino."

"Quite, They're too small. So the observer influences the observed, according to, or perhaps in an amount proportional to, the amount of measurement."

"You could say," said Phil, "that nothing exists until I look at it."

"If you were an existentialist, yes; or a dream merchant."

Phil nodded sagely. "So what?"

"So what if information barons have an enormous influence just by virtue of possession?"

"Er... how?"

"It's impossible to work out on a macro scale. I'm seeing if I can apply a physical law of the microverse to another situation."

"What if you could?"

"Oh, it would just confirm what we know already. People, organisations, with vast databases have a lot of power over everyone."

"Before they even do anything with it?"

"It would prove that; yes."

"Like the Vatican?"

"They and the Illuminati, through the confessional, of course."

"Does it?" asked Phil, looking at the paper's jumble of figures.

"'Dunno. I ought to leave it for my spare time really," said Robert. "Take it home. It'll keep me out of mischief, anyway."

What *could* the fractaerial do? Robert decided to widen his options by obtaining a high power UHF television amplifier for it. Really its physical position was of no consequence. Once focused on the den he could control it through the data link just as if it had been sitting on the bench before him. It was quite safe there really, and, with the new amplifier, cheaper on electricity.

He started a new series of experiments, bringing the wave to a sharper and sharper focus. What if he were to make it reappear in five dimensions rather than three? His first transmission had necessarily focused on a fairly broad area, as he did not know the precise, exact position of the new TV aerial on his roof. A little experience however, had allowed him to pinpoint the beam quite accurately. He now needed only a thousandth the transmission power between lab and den.

Aware to some extent of the brightness of the fire he was playing with, Robert bought a small wooden picnic table from Williams' Garden Centre on Woolton Road, and focused his attentions on that from a safe vantage point behind the den's window. Transmissions to the roof aerial remained at minimum power. It seemed the radion't had virtually no transmission loss. He potted up a sprig of floribunda and placed it in the centre of the table.

Had he asked himself what he expected, the answer might have been fire, some sort of explosion. But, as he washed the soil from his hands, he told himself he expected nothing. Or anything. His had to be a purely objective and scientific mind.

With less awe and ceremony than the occasion later turned out to have deserved, he typed the command and hit return.

"Poof," went the plant, pot and all, in an instantaneous flash of colour. Robert scrunched his eyes and looked again. It was not there. He ran downstairs and out to where it had stood. No sign of anything. 'Strange' seemed something of an understatement. The experiment had consisted of a one kilowatt blast of signal, programmed to reappear in five, not three dimensions. Duration one second.

Shocked, stunned and speechless, even to Felix, Robert returned to the Den. For want of anything better to do, he repeated the command.

"Poof," went the plant. It was back, large as life, real as he. Throwing caution and scientific method to the wind, he zapped it again, refocused on a corner of the den, and blasted it back into existence not ten feet from where he was sitting.

He looked at it very closely. It was quite rational to believe his own eyes, surely, but *could he*? This was too small. He could have blacked out and carried it up.

He selected the Olivetti's co-ordinate map and moved a cross-hair target across a digitised representation of the garden. "Click," went the mouse on a section of border. He pulled down a micro-menu and adjusted focus volume. Across the screen, and up a simulated storey, he focused on the den co-ordinates once more. Tap. Click. Pouf. Zap! He blinked. Twice. Then burst out laughing. The whole floribunda plant had been surgically removed from the end of the garden, and now reposed in a corner of the room, blocking the door. A bee, then several other insects rose from the mass of stalks, leaves and fading red, flying round the room. He walked over to it, giggling like a child, and let a ladybird crawl off a leaf onto his outstretched finger. Immense! Crucial! Magic!

He walked to the opened window and shook the charmed creature away. What now? A stream of possibilities rushed through his mind. He shrugged, looked about the room in wonder again and giggled his way past the huge plant to the door. Hmm, Teletransportation. Had a nice ring to it. He staggered his way down to the lounge, stuck Handel's 'Messiah' on the turntable, poured himself a large Scotch and collapsed in a chair to the awesome, familiar opening bars.

13   DISASTER

The way her coat hung down reminded Jane of something, she couldn't quite figure what. Her mind, in this heightened state of awareness, seemed to see connections and significances in lots of things recently. And how was she today? Feeling good, strong, excited. It was an 'up' day. The downs of the past week or two were not especially memorable this morning.

"Good morning Jane," enunciated Miss Dwight, making her jump. God, that woman was spooky. She turned to face the intruder.

"Hello Kathleen."

"Could you see the Professor? He wants a few words with you."

For some reason Jane felt a lump of confidence in her throat sink to her bottom. Even if Miss Dwight were incapable of sounding otherwise, this sounded forbiddingly formal. It deviated from the routine.

"What, now?" she asked, stupidly.

"Yes."

Jane trod her way to the office gingerly, with trepidation.

"Ah, Jane." He welcomed her warmly, like that first interview. Miss Dwight entered with pen and notepad from a side door and seated herself.

"I'm sorry to have to say this, but you're fired."

'He feels sorry,' she thought, irrelevantly. 'A man of compassion, emotion.' "You've had rather more unexplained sick leave than a new member of staff may be allowed." She gulped. "The quality of your work, excellent at first, has been steadily declining. Mary and Margaret have been forced to take on more and more of your workload. You have been a disruptive influence on the work of the hospital." He handed her an envelope. Jane felt numb and sick. "Your written dismissal and P45."

Now she did not feel anything. She might have said something. Events might have transpired. She left with the package. She probably walked straight to Dave's, certainly ended up there.

He looked up from a magazine. "Oh, Hi."

"Hi Dave."

She stood, uncomfortably, waiting for a couple of humanoid snails to finish their survival preparations for World War Three. They left.

"Dave ..."

"Jane, I've got something to tell you."

He spoke from a face that had aged maybe ten years.

"Dave, I can't ..."

"Jane, stop. I've been trying for ..."

He put his hands together, interlacing the thin fingers, then cracked them.

"It's ... Oh let's close up for a minute." He came out from behind the counter, brushed past her and turned a sign over, snapped the door's catch.

Desperately, "What?"

"Jane, I can't handle you any more." She could see he was explaining something serious, another nasty shock. And then she wasn't looking into his face. She could see them both, standing amongst the jars and packets on the shelves. He was sitting against the front of the counter, she, against the freezer in the middle of the shop floor, a long way down.

He started to speak again, incredibly slowly. It was like a film. The two figures shrank, down a long tunnel. "You're like a wild thing. I don't understand you any more. I love you but I can't get through. You're somewhere else. It's all just a world of games to you. I can't keep up with the drugs, the mad ideas... I, I'm losing myself."

Her figure put out an arm towards him. "You can't just... I love you too. You can't go."

"Give it a while to heal Jane. See you in a month or two. Maybe we can still be friends."

"I don't. I don't..?"

She turned and struggled with the door catch; suddenly she was back down there with him and it was too close, suffocating. She wrenched the door open and ran out, blankly, across the busy road. Cars swerved and braked and blared their horns. She was running, she knew not where.

__14__ CRISIS COMBINATION

He stepped through the sliding doors and raised a hand to Josella, who smilingly lifted hers in reply. She sat behind an expanse of mahogany, the palm trees behind her setting off nicely her translucent blue blouse. In his journey through the development suite, he was surprised to see everyone swivel round to stare at him. He made a movement towards Phil, then backed away. Phil had turned back to face his terminal, refused to meet his eye. As he retreated, stepping backwards, he was stopped by an arm around his shoulder.

"Robert, old boy," said Colin, "we know what you're up to. You can't be trusted. I'm afraid... it's all over."

With nothing less than utter terror, he slowly turned to face the speaker. Colin was standing next to one of the directors. They both wore khaki double breasted suits, with matching ties he instinctively knew to proclaim membership of the same masonic lodge. On either side of them stood immaculately robed Arab princes, head-dresses rippling in a warm breeze. To their sides, olive-skinned paramilitaries had silently crept up, crouching, to aim their stubby sub-machine guns at his head.

"No!" he screamed. "It wasn't…"

Colin lifted a finger and pointed at him, indicating that he should remain silent. "Our friends need this technology Robert. They have paid for its development. It is of crucial importance to them and us." He gestured with outstretched palms, as if pleading. "We have to protect our economic, not to mention military interests."

Robert sprang forward. "You cheating bastard! Traitor!" But Colin slipped through his grasp like a wraith, and he was alone with the Arabs on the sand. The thugs advanced on him as he lay, helpless and stunned, hot sun beating down on his balding head.

"It is you who is the thief, Mr Ashley" spoke one prince, a sheikh, he supposed. "While working under our employ, your creations belong to us." He made a gesture to the gunmen. "And no-one else." As he spoke, they raised their weapons and began to beat him, striking his arms and head with hard steel. He cried out, screaming, writhing, struggling to avoid the heavy blows.

Something soft was in his way. He grappled with it and became entangled. It was tying him in knots, trapping, folding over and over, like… his duvet. His breath came in short gasps. This was his bed. He was sweating profusely. He was awake.

*   *   *

Jane lifted her head up from the hands that clasped it. Thinking about her problems only seemed to make them more intractable. She felt locked in vicious circles of paranoia with no way out. Looking at the telephone she stepped again through a mental address book. Whom could she turn to now? Anyone? To trust with her life?

Really, as a last resort, there was no one else. Resolute, she dialled the number, stopped half way through. Of course, he would be at work. She picked up the phone book and flicked through, her earnest fingers running down the list of names. Puzzled, she stopped between two entries. It wasn't there. Had someone tampered with her directory? Reprinted the vital page? Someone who *knew*? A fresh sense of foreboding started to worry and gnaw at her mind. No, the firm did secret work; it had to be ex-directory.

As she closed the book, a pattern of lines showed itself at the paper's edges. Stupid! This was the new improved(!) directory. Business lines listed separately. She opened it again and quickly found the number; dialled.

Her call was answered after a few rings:

"Good morning GEC Plessey Crypto. Hello?"

Jane composed herself. "Hello. Could I speak to Robert Ashley, please?" After a short interlude of tinny tune she was connected.

"Hello?"

"Hi Rob, it's Jane."

"Hi Jane. How 'you doing?"

"Oh, not too well."

"What's up?"

"Oh...problems."

He tutted. "Ah, Jane. Look, I'm a mite busy at the moment. Do you want to come round tonight for a meal? It's been ages."

"Yes, I would like that. I'll bring some wine. I can't tell you on the phone anyway."

"Eightish?"

"Seven?"

"OK, see you then."

"'Bye." They replaced their receivers, both looking out of their respective windows for a while, wondering what revelations the evening would bring; what to tell. Robert was feeling decidedly uneasy himself after the morning's still-vivid nightmare.

The day wore on slowly. They prepared for the re-union with an edge of nervous anticipation. Robert dusted off his vegetarian recipe book (a Christmas present from Jane) and dug deep into the freezer. Eventually they were all prepared. Robert surveyed his bubbling pots; Jane sat, bouncing in the black cab, fare in her sticky fist.

She arrived and pressed the doorbell; he answered almost at once. She stepped in; they kissed, briefly.

"I'm making something from your Christmas present Jane."

"My what? Oh I see. Mmm. Smells good."

He took her jacket and hung it on the end of the stairs.

"So, what have you been up to?" asked Jane.

"Me? Er, lots of boring secret stuff."

"Secrets are never boring – Warmonger."

"Jane, you know it's only tarted-up telephones."

"Yeah, I know," she sighed wearily.

"And how are you?"

"Shagged out. Knackered. Destroyed. Just lost my job and my boyfriend."

"What, all at once?"

"Yes"

"That was a bit careless, wasn't it?"

"Unsympathetic git."

"Any connection?"

"I suppose so."

He tried to cheer her up. "Well, you're here now, with me to look after you. Just relax. Have a drink, something to eat. Stay the night if you like. The spare room's made up. I can give you a lift in the morning."

"Where to?"

"Oh yes, no job. Sorry. Home. Wherever." He shrugged.

"Rob, you're wonderful. I couldn't wish for a better brother." She produced a bottle of Lambrusco from her bag.

He guided her into the lounge where Mozart's Clarinet Concerto was reaching its final movement. "And I couldn't wish for a sweeter sister. Here, I'll put this in the fridge for later." He turned the volume down. "What do you want now? Whisky, wine, a beer?"

"Whisky please," she sniffled.

He took the wine out to the kitchen, checked dinner and returned to pour two generous tumblers of The Macallan then found Jane an ashtray. They sat, she on the sofa, he in the armchair next to her, savouring nectar of liquid – sound.

"I really loved Dave. Now I've lost both of them, I didn't really care for the job so much. He was so kind and caring. I thought we might..."

"Go on, you'll find another fella soon enough."

"What about you? You've not been going out with anyone since Gloria in Cambridge. That was years ago."

"I've been out with a few girl friends. I just don't want them taking over yet, that's all."

"Mmm." She understood Robert like that very well.

They filled in the rough details of their lives since last Christmas's family reunion. By the end of Robert's excellent ratatouille and four bottles of Belgian bier, he had confessed to alienation and extreme overwork, she, to nervous breakdown and a moderate degree of drug addiction. They held hands across the table for a moment of hope before clearing away the dishes.

Jane started the real discussion in the kitchen as she took a plate from her brother. She waved the teacloth at it in a feeble sort of way. "Rob, one of the last games I was playing was about you."

"Me! A character in a game?"

"Yes. D&D – Dungeons and Dragons," she explained.

"What happened to me?"

"Well, I'll have to explain how I rolled you up first. I picked the alignment – neutral, chaotic, then..."

"What do you mean, chaotic?" asked Robert, obviously riled.

"Oh, it's just a way of playing. It allows you to have more exciting adventures."

"I see," he Josella-ed at her.

She continued: "Then I had to roll an n-sided die for each of your attributes."

"Attributes? Like what?"

She counted off her fingers one by one. "Strength, intelligence, life-power, charm, endurance, magic, you know."

"So what was I? A Rambo midget?"

"A chess playing wizard", she revealed through grinning white teeth.

"But I don't even play chess." Robert's upper lip quavered as he tried in vain to control an irrepressible chortle. "So, what, ha, happened to me?"

"You completed your Quest," she replied, hanging up the tea towel.

He followed her back into the lounge. "Which was?"

"Was? Oh, to find a gateway into another world."

His face fell. "What did you just say?"

"Find a gateway into another world."

He sat down suddenly. "I thought that was it. What makes you say that?"

"It's just what I picked, the roll of the dice, what would fit the game scenario."

"Oh."

There were a few minutes of awkward silence, which Robert eventually broke by putting on a rather clever and arty ambient music LP.

"When did the game start?"

"About a month ago."

"Ah!" He relaxed for some reason and found them more drinks. "An interesting coincidence. Cheers."

"Coincidence? About what?"

"Something I can't really say."

"Ah, an official secret."

"A personal one. I can't really say to anyone. Except, perhaps, someone I could trust with my life."

"That's a bit melodramatic isn't it?"

"Not really. Your life could be in danger too."

"Now you've got to tell me."

"I haven't, but I don't suppose there's anyone else. And I can't keep it to myself for ever.

Jane, I've invented a teleport machine."

"Rob, that's wonderful!" She went over and gave him a massive hug. Embarrassed, he acquiesced. Eventually they disentangled.

"I can move objects and living forms from A to B, anywhere, instantaneously!"

"Wow! What's the problem?"

"You seem to be taking this relatively calmly," he noted. "Most people would think I was a complete nutter."

"Maybe you are. Let's see it then."

"OK. Follow me." He jerked his head as if to pull her up.

She followed him up to the lab, heart beating like a sledgehammer, attempted a whistle, then stood transfixed in awe. Crossing the threshold from the landing definitely took her into another world. It stood quite apart from any sort of domesticity. Along the back window lay an expansive black work bench, wall to wall. On it, various grey plastic receptacles offered neat arrangements of office consumables. The Olivetti sat, sinister; to the right were Hewlett Packard spectrum analyser, Apple laser printer and fax. The walls were covered in shelf disk- and book-cases holding an impressive scientific library.

Along the wall shared with the Smiths was a full array of nineteen inch equipment racks. A shelf jutted out at waist height holding assorted keyboards, mixers, pads and devices virtually unclassifiable by function. Hidden amongst a busily cluttered jungle of facias sat a discrete CD system, and along part of their upper range was a row of colour monitors. Jane looked up at a triplicate array of cartoon men in close-up, shaving. Along the bottom of each screen was the word 'shasim', and a rapidly incrementing time display. The heads turned in unison, inspecting pixels of stubble, threw water, splayed foam and drew smooth pink lines of pink on white with their virtual razors, upped and downed head angle, concluding with the mandatory and magnificently realistic cut of adam's apple. The fancy had come to Rob while shaving, obviously. He supposed it was Max Headroom inspired. Next thing, he was setting up a video camera in the bathroom, timing, digitising himself. A good buzz.

While Jane had been looking round and round in bewilderment, he had plugged himself into the terminal, and was scrolling through pages of data, letters, symbols and graphics, speaking as he punched keys. The cartoon men smiled politely, nodded and blanked out.

"I'm not really one of your evil animal research boys y' know, but I did move those rhododendron up here and back." He gestured towards the floribunda, out of the window. Jane moved over and looked. "A few insects came for the ride and they seem to be all right still." He pointed again to a leafy covered fish tank by the window. It contained sprigs of the bush, crawling with an assortment of arthropods. "Anyway, I'll just do a simple hop for you now."

Deftly he unclasped his wristwatch and placed it on a clear area of the workbench. A key tap later it vanished, reappearing a few feet to the right.

Jane clapped in appreciation.

"You're a genius! And a magician. Can you do it further?"

Robert shrugged, gave a quizzical smile and opened a small wooden drawer below the workbench. "Happy Christmas

Moonbeam," he said, taking out a small rock and placing it in her palm.

"Moon rock! You've been to the moon?!?"

"Well not personally. I just sent a TV camera to look for pretty things."

Jane searched for somewhere to collapse; finally settled for the floor, turned the gem over and over, gloating.

Rob flicked through a thick and glossy book; passed her that as well. "There you are. Just like the pictures."

"Nice one" she nodded, running out of superlatives for the moment.

Demonstration over, Robert suggested they go back downstairs.

Jane tried to recover back on the sofa while he stood to speak, pacing back and forth a little.

"So, it's all very well having this fabulous toy, but I've got no idea what the hell to do with it. It's making me completely paranoid too."

"Why not just sell it?" asked Jane. "Patent it, retire, and go on holiday to interesting places."

"Ha!" he retorted. "Sell it? Who to? Oil, motors, airlines, wiped out overnight. Telecoms, power, tourism turned head over heels. Jane, this virtually makes the wheel obsolete."

"Oh yeah, mmm. I suppose it does really. Couldn't we use it to help people? Like.. zapping food mountains to Africa? Radioactive waste into outer space? Huh?"

"Possibly." He shrugged. "Mainly I'm afraid of the wrong people finding out about it. People who might – lose out – by its introduction. They'd just kill me and suppress it. Use it..."

"Kill us."

"Ah yes, kill us."

"It could be good for the planet, though. No more cars or planes wrecking the ozone layer. Just teleport depots."

"Which planet?" asked Robert

Jane frowned. "Oh I see! We can go anywhere ... yes."

They contemplated the possibilities in silence for a moment.

"People could commute from anywhere ..."

"No more borders ..."

"... or countries ..."

"What about privacy?" asked Jane.

"Or security?"

"The power's frightening. It's mind-blowing!"

"Constant solar power... We can't begin to imagine the possibilities", stated Robert sensibly. "Or for that matter, the practical difficulties involved in using it properly. What we need to do is ..." He sat down and refilled their tumblers. "... set up a field trial. See how reliable the technology is, what we can use it for on a small scale, gauge the ..."

"Guinea pig!" interrupted Jane. "You want me to be the guinea pig. Your own sister." She glared as best she could.

"Yes" admitted Robert with disarming charm. "I do, actually, if you wouldn't mind. Big risks. Inconceivable gains. You've never been on an adventure like this before, have you?"

She had to admit, she hadn't. "You could live anywhere. Commute wherever. There wouldn't be any distinction of place, like, like er ..."

"no individuality of location", finished Robert.

"Like melting an oil painting, mixing all the colours together into grey."

"Hmm." Robert was non-committal. "We're just speculating. There's nothing to go on till we've got some experience. I thought maybe we could set up a trading company – import/export with no shipping costs."

"Or V.A.T. That sounds all right," said Jane, sitting up.

"We could rent a base overseas, rent a warehouse or something..."

"Zap the stuff back here and sell it," concluded Jane. "Cosmic smuggling. Sound."

"The question being, what to trade. I was thinking of computer parts possibly, from Taiwan."

"Sell computer parts?" asked Jane, incredulous. "With servicing and invoices and serial numbers? On the blag? You know, sometimes, for a genius, you're pretty thick."

Robert's ego blew up and popped. He sat back, defeated, deflated. "You're quite right. In fact for an unemployed schizo girly you have remarkable insight. Any more ideas?"

"Fruit."

"Imbecile.

Jane sighed out slowly. "Not – you – dear – brother. We can trade fresh tropical fruit or vegetables. Mangoes, oranges, pineapples, tomatoes... I've got all the connections."

"Who?"

"Well, there's Dave..."

Robert started nodding. "I like it. The goods can't be traced and we'll have a natural advantage over our competitors. Ours will be the freshest and the cheapest. We need a cover. In both countries. A van, a building and an apparent local wholesale business."

"One of us here, one there."

"No. You'll have to start it off, with my help. I have to continue my job for the moment," he explained. "I don't have the resources for further development myself, and I don't want to appear to act suspiciously. It will look like I'm helping you get back on your feet and start your own business, which I am.

"So, where do you want to go shopping?"

Jane seemed to think for a moment, smirked, hesitated. "India?"

"OK" he agreed. "You've always wanted to go, haven't you."

"Yes."

ANGELS CHÍC

ARJUNA KRISHNA-DAS

PART TWO
SELENE

*As the day began, Siddhartha asked
his host, the ferryman, to take him across
the river. The ferryman took him across on
his bamboo raft. The broad sheet of water
glimmered pink in the light of the morning.*

*'It is a very beautiful river,'
he said to his companion.*

*'Yes,' said the ferryman, 'it is a very
beautiful river. I love it above everything.
I have often listened to it, gazed at it, and
I have always learned something from
it. One can learn much from a river.'*

Hermann Hesse – Siddhartha

1   Eastern Delight

Emirates flight 217 was cruising smoothly at fifteen thousand feet, approaching Delhi International Airport. The pilot, a handsomely greying and paunchy Birmingham expatriate, finished a terse dialogue with what passed for air traffic control in this part of the world, reached up for a switch in the Airbus's crowded cockpit and began descent. Twenty seats back, Jane looked dreamily out of the window at the wonderfully alien countryscape below. She heard the captain's announcement and instructions about seat belts and cigarettes. As the plane banked into a turn, she could distantly see, but not yet smell, the sprawling metropolis. With her destination now in sight, a host of feelings pushed their way into her mind – strength, wonder, freedom... and the purpose of the trip, solidified, a mere plan no longer. A dull ache grew in her ears as the cabin depressurised; she tried valiantly to gulp. Little tears of salt were trickling down her cheeks. She did not brush them away, savouring the feelings they sprang from.

What a wonderful way to travel, she thought. I hope Rob doesn't make all this obsolete. Below her she saw fields of suburbia, crawling bee-cars, dot-people, and the edge of a corrugated shanty-ville.

The plane banked again and began its final descending approach, engines changing their pitch to a more urgent tone. The ground, in a grey tarmac jacket, rushed up to meet it, flying past at a dizzying pace. And then they touched, a small jolt, air smooth turned on wheels, the sound and feel of the engines' reverse thrust, feeling of having arrived; taxiing; stopped.

'Ding-dong' chimed speakers as the no smoke – yo belts light extinguished. She and her fellow travellers disembarked onto a bus not much smaller than the plane. It sped them to the terminal, where Jane was greeted by a gargantuan Ganesh, eventually recovered her luggage from the creaking conveyer, passed through customs, and had her passport perfunctorily stamped.

Quadrilingual flight announcements filled the vast, crowded concourse. She filtered through a horde of would-be porters and stepped out through automatic doors, into real heat and severe sunshine. A line of taxis stood waiting, dusty remnants of Austin and other antique designs. The drivers besieged her, until, after some hectic bargaining, she picked one and was away.

"The er... " She reached for a scrap of paper in her purse. "Manzil hotel please, ..Bombay street East." She would soon find out if Delta Travel back on Leece Street knew their stuff on hotels. They did on taxis. Her driver guided the cab along slip roads to a wide boulevard lined with palm trees, flower beds and lush grass. As the motor speeded up, Jane relaxed back in her seat, fanning herself, and just enjoyed the journey. A thousand smells, exotic and all-too-familiar, streamed through their open windows. The expressway met a roundabout and split up. Now she saw the sights drooled over in books and travel brochures for so long: street markets, rickshaws, a glimpse of a snake charmer, temples, mysterious narrow alleyways, people, and more people everywhere.

They thronged the streets and pavements like so many variegated ants. Fat, thin, businessmen, beggars, mothers, children, hustlers, old, holy, noisy, slow: foreign. An enjoyable culture shock so far.

The Manzil turned out to be an imposing relic of colonialism. Jane guessed that the very reasonable rate she had been quoted in sterling could easily be decimated by a move to less luxurious surroundings later.

For the moment, though, she revelled in it, from the moment the case wallah took her luggage in from the taxi. She signed the register in a film-set style marble lobby cooled by giant ceiling fans, then followed the porter up sweeping stairs to her room on the second floor. It looked out on a dazzling back garden, delights of living colour bursting out around the central fountain.

She leaned back against the door and took in the room. It had a double bed, phone, pine wardrobe and chest of drawers, doors to a balcony and en-suite shower room. Good. Magnificent, in fact. She slipped her clothes off with great relief, and stepped inside, revelling in a cold shower until her whole body was goosepimply and shivering. Soap and shampoo well rinsed, she turned it off at last, dripped into the room and sat on a towel draped over the bed. For the next half hour, her good humour evaporated with the water on her back as she tried in vain to contact Robert by local operator. Eventually she gave up and used the Radion't. He was in.

"Hi Jane. Everything OK?"

"Hi Rob. Everything except the phone. I should have used this straight away."

"No use using a sledgehammer to crack a nut unless you have to. What's it like, anyway?"

"Well, the flight was great. Took off twice." She moaned sensuously. Taxi tried to rip me off as predicted. It's as hot as hell here, and I could seriously consider living in this wonderful hotel. It's mega. Never seen anything like it."

"Shall I pop over?"

"No! I've got no clothes on. And you've had no jabs. Wait 'till I've got the shack, fathead."

"Any plans?"

"Fermenting in the cobwebby recesses of my brain."

"I see. Well stay off the hard stuff and good luck. Keep in touch."

"You too. 'Bye."

They disconnected.

She placed the handset back on the bedside table, lowered her head and began to sleep off her five and a half hour jet lag.

_2_   FEET, BUSES AND FAKIRS

Jane awoke suddenly, fully conscious, highly alive, feeling good. She had neither smuggled nor indulged in liquid duty frees on Robert's strict orders; as a result, her head was clear, her mind racing with receding dreams, germinating ideas and plans. Coughing her lungs clear too, she reached for a cigarette and lit it. There would not be much time for sightseeing. Since that fateful evening, three weeks ago, Rob had more or less taken charge of her life. Paradoxically, simultaneously restricting and liberating. She had left her flat for the moment, told friends she was off to the East and moved into his spare room. All that weird stuff with players controlling things was gently receding. The few times she had rung Dave, he hadn't been overjoyed, but seemed glad she was getting it together anyway. He promised to buy a few things when they started trading.

She slunk out of bed, into the shower. Jet fresh luxury. Enjoy it while you can, she thought, aware of hardships to come soon with simple village life. Rob, uncomprehending 'Indian time', had prepared her a virtually hour-by hour itinerary which now seemed to be somehow missing from her luggage. Hopefully, nothing important was with it.

Stepped out, dried and dressing, Jane again heard the exotic ambient soundscape of birds, crowds, bells, dogs and cars. From the sounds, and sun over the garden, she guessed it was mid-morning. Her watch confirmed the time as she pulled the strap tight. 10.40 am. A place like this should still be doing breakfast. She glided downstairs. It was. Nor was she alone as she took her wicker seat in the lavish marble dining room. Scattered groups of businesslike-looking guests munched and sipped their way through baskets of croissants, cereal and coffee. Real India, it seemed, lay well outside the Manzil.

After noon she attempted a leisurely stroll through the down-town markets and sights. A porter had suggested that she head towards Connaught Park. Prepared with only wide hat and sunglasses, Jane was unready for the midday heat. The streets were less crowded, and shops closed for the sun-wary to take siesta. Washing lines hung everywhere, laden with light cloth. The buildings they were attached to appeared to have been placed randomly, one on top of another.

With no shade on either side of the wide, dusty street, Jane began to pall. Her head ached; her breathing was like an act of fire-eating. Her clothes seemed glued to her. She was being orbited by groups and swarms of variously annoying insects, from the midges and mosquitoes close by, through flies, to a persistent rabble of young children, half-dressed, laughing, pointing, jeering, speaking, hands out, grabbing.

She saw her chance a block away. Bright and garish, like all Indo-tech, noisy even above the street's clamour, there was no mistaking it. Nor the small group awaiting its appearance. It choked its way to stop beside just as she reached them, clambered on and squeezed herself into a space between one passenger's elbow and another's foot, clutching her hat so it would not be lost. The bus moved on again, hangers-on hanging on in a cloud of dust and smoke.

They came to a park and she alighted. If this wasn't it she didn't care. There was shade and grass and a place to put her head down. She found a spot and collapsed with relief beneath a clump of palm trees. Started. One of the children following her was still there. Impossible. A boy, maybe not a child... fourteen, fifteen? Was it him? She was not sure. It couldn't be. He was left behind, someone else. He noticed her look, stopped chewing for a moment, gave her a chilling smirk, turned, lost himself in another crowd.

Jane felt lost herself. And uneasy. She needed a drink. Everyone was staring at her, especially the men. She rose, picked her shoes up and made for a kiosk nearby. It turned out to be an entrance to an underground shopping arcade. First, she found a cafe and rehydrated. The place served chai and ice cream in slices. Her physical discomfort was eased at once, her anxiety she tried to push slowly to the back of her mind. Realisation of their revolutionary plans kept crystallising in an ever-more complete form.

Via browsing through trinkets, souvenir and clothes shops, Jane came to the arcade's other end, resolved to investigate native dress further soon.

She left the park and began exploring shady alleyways, labyrinths of twisting turns. Everywhere was the shout and cry of children, barrow boys, bells, carts, horns and footfalls. Beggars and traders sat with their backs to rough apartment buildings, merchandise or disability arrayed before them on cloths and rugs. Here and there Jane stopped, holding still against the pushing throng to try on a ring, examine an unfamiliar item, leaf through an occasional book. This stuff was being given away. Why shouldn't they do rings, clothes, jewellery too? Maybe a bit of incense? In places, the sky nearly disappeared between the high reaching verandas. At one point, the human sea parted as an itinerant and bony cow meandered through the lane, kicking up dust. Jane placed a hand on her heart, laughing. This was really cool, a better place. She followed the cow with her eye, then froze. Was that him? A small boy with a hard gaze, chewing something. The sweat turned cold on her. Avoid trouble, said a soft inner voice. She looked ahead. A pair of stout wooden doors stood open, beckoning. A temple of some kind. She walked forward and stepped inside.

It was cool, calm, and seemed very dark at first. Her eyes adjusted as she walked down a bare hallway to the back of the building. Street noise subsided; she could hear another sound – a repetitive phrase, sung, in unison, sweetly. It came from behind another door. Next to it was a shoe rack, piled high with sandals. Jane took hers off and stepped inside.

Froze with shock. Déjà vu or new? Mind raced. Senses struggled with sensations, smells, sounds, the Sight, and something else. "Chalumba Yeh"

She sat down with the fifty or so others. An old lady with a toddler on her lap leaned over to a heap of cushions and span one to her, smiling. "Kali-ma, Kali-ma, Kali-ma" Jane smiled and nodded back, returned her gaze to the Deity figure, focus of worship. "Chalumba-Yeh!" Smoky camphor lamps surrounded her. She stood tall behind an open curtain and roller. "Kali-ma, Kali-ma, Kali-ma." Smaller figures stood around, and the whitewashed wall behind her was graced with pictures of noble, play- and fearful looking gods.

The Deity Herself, dark and awesome, stood a good seven feet high. Around her neck, a colourful flower garland was draped. Her eyes ablaze, her mouth open to reveal a long red tongue, she wielded a large machete in one of her four hands; the hand below it clasped a trident. Her upper left hand held a disembodied head by its hair, the lower, a vessel, presumably to catch the drips of blood. Around her neck was a garland of skulls. Her breasts bare, she was clothed only in a skirt of leg bones.

Jane sat cross-legged behind the other women on their side of the temple. Her spirits were lifted by the atmosphere, and even if she didn't join in the chanting, it seemed to do her head some good. When it eventually stopped, she bowed with the rest of them, praying for safe passage under her breath.

The congregation rose, mingled and chatted on their way out. The old lady came over and tried to talk, but they didn't get beyond a few signs. Her daughter, the baby's mother, was a fluent English speaker.

Jane was on her own in Delhi? Staying in a hotel? On business?

They introduced themselves on the way out, Parvatti, Sita and Lakshmi in descending order of age, then Jane found herself invited back for a meal. Relieved to find herself in friendly female company, she accepted at once.

The family visited Kali's temple most afternoons.

Jane commended the ceremony, but questioned Kali's gory form. Sita responded, talking of her in terms of the Divine Mother, extolling her as the great purifier. She placed a hand on Jane's arm.

"You feel the shakti, yes?"

Jane supposed she did.

"That is from her. She is a great devotee of the Lord, in charge of the material energy."

Their home was a crowded couple of rooms in a nearby apartment building, rough but clean. Jane played with baby Lakshmi while Parvatti and Sita got busy with long-simmering pans. The meal of spicy dhal with rice and chapattis they served was tasty; Jane ate more than her fill. Grandfather and Sita's husband sat to be served a little apart from the women, talking in Hindi.

Jane stayed until mid-evening, making friends with Sita, learning a few tips about life in the city.

Over the next week, she visited them a few more times. Sita persuaded her to buy a sari, and showed her how to wear it. After that, she had less trouble with letching men and begging children. Her list of likely merchandise grew, as did her desire to get out into the country. Rob kept in touch by radion't, and approved of her plans for a buying expedition.

"Great idea! Take a bus. Just buy what you know you can sell, and only if it's dirt cheap."

"What about moving out completely into the country?" she asked.

"Stay small, stay in the city and don't get noticed," he replied. "Ideally, you need to rent somewhere first. Preferably with a front and back door."

"What about insects? Did you see that film The Fly, where the guy materialised in the way of a fly and got a head transplant? I like my head. I'm used to it. Dave used to say it was one of my prettier bits."

"I didn't bother seeing the film, but I heard about it. Actually I don't think materialising in the way of a load of air molecules was too good for the plants and insects. There's a way round it of course. I've just programmed in some new routines. Basically it's just like moving counters in the tower of Brahma puzzle. If I'm travelling from A to B, I have to move a body-sized chunk of air up a few miles from B to C first, after a telescan, to make sure I don't lobotomise some poor airline pilot with a bumble bee. Then I have to transfer myself immediately, A to B, and move another chunk of air from D, above A to A itself in order to prevent an implosion of vacuum, in the lab for instance."

"Oh!" exclaimed Jane. "We have to clear a space before we land then fill in the hole after we jump."

"Exactly. We can also telescan possible landing sites with a radion't TV camera to check for unwanted observers or other hazards."

"Wouldn't you lobotomise the airline pilot with this TV camera, and wouldn't unwanted observers see it?"

"Different types of telescan, Jane. The teledensity scan doesn't need a camera; the camera telescan only takes a few milliseconds."

"Why go up a few miles? Why not just swap air with traveller, B to A?"

"Because, as you reminded me, I haven't had any jabs. This way lessens the risk of transferring disease-carrying pests."

"And what about aiming the aerial? I don't want to be lost in some clammy hyperspace void while it's turning round to point at somewhere else."

"The fractaerial is aimed and focused electronically, Jane, just like modern radar. Haven't you been on a ship's bridge recently?"

She treated the question rhetorically. "Well, that seems quite straightforward. When are you coming over?"

"When are you renting a telepad?"

"Oh, a telepad! That does better than a shack, doesn't it?"

"Well?"

"When I've been round the countryside a bit. We can have the telepad here in Delhi but I'd like to get out of it as much as possible."

"You'd better not. Remember last time, crazy people running the world."

"They do."

"Last thing we need is paranoia and conspiracy theories. Watch it."

"Don't you start" she ordered back, hurt. "I can look after myself. Don't worry."

But he did. His little sister and partner thousands of miles away, doing a difficult, dangerous job, alone.

They said goodbye, put their handsets down. Robert looked out of the lab's window thoughtfully for a moment or two. Was the strain showing on him? Shrugging a shoulder, he turned back to the psychedelic snowflake patterns unfurling in ever greater detail on the screens in front of him. He was exploring the colourful spirals and sea-horse tails of Mandelbrot's fractal set.

Insistently he returned to his keyboard, tap, tap, tap dancing.

3   RAJPUR VILLAGE

For a short time more, Jane stayed stuck in the city. Everything was hot, sticky, crowded and dirty. Almost worst of all was the attention she generated. Countless pairs of eyes swivelled her way, letching, envying, desiring her lithe body.

Eventually she had had enough, contracted a mild sickness and took to lying in her room or the blissfully calm garden. The young Bengali waiters would bring her endless cups of chai and lemonade, as she half-read train timetables, or a book she had discovered in some downtown bazaar.

'Now I know how a cow feels,' she thought, one hazy afternoon by the fountain. Three or four flies crept intently on her arms and legs; she couldn't even raise the energy to swish her tail at them.

The next day, or perhaps the one after, Jane took her leave of the Manzil, paid her bill to the manager, a wiry old man with more hair on his upper lip than the rest of his head put together, and caught a rickshaw through early-morning cool to the Interstate bus terminal. There, she found a bus heading South and boarded it, cursing her inability to simply teleport over the country.

Her seat was on the right, by the window, near the front. The other seats soon filled up with assorted travellers. Amongst the Indians were a few lighter faces from Europe and the West. One stopped to lodge his cases on the rack above Jane's head. He sat down beside her. Jane double took slightly. He wasn't Indian, but he dressed like one. Like a *sadhu*, or holy man in fact, judging from his saffron *kirta* and *dhoti*. His head was shaved bald except for a knotted tuft at the back; his forehead was decorated with a long yellow "V" looking rather like a tuning fork, and his feet were bare, having just vacated a pair of open sandals. Around his neck hung a fist-sized bag. Jane guessed that was for meditation beads.

The driver boarded, fiddling with coins and tickets in his waist bag. He took out a few joss sticks and lit them with the first strike of a spluttering match. Placing them in a holder before a picture on the dashboard, he clasped his hands for a moment as if praying for safe deliverance of the bus and its passengers, then swung into his seat and started the engine. It screeched, banged and rattled into a state of wild animation. They were off.

Jane glanced again at her odd companion. He noticed, nodded, put a hand in his bead bag and moved it from around his head to his lap.

"Hi. Are you going to *Vrindavan*?" he asked.

"Uh, no. *Rajpur.*"

"That's not so far." He spoke in a soft American drawl.

"No."

The bus hit a pothole, and lurched, bouncing violently. Jane held onto to the seat in front, cursing the road. She saw now why the driver needed so much faith in prayer. Her companion too, it seemed; her guess was right. He was shaking the bag on his hand, chanting softly, very fast, in a sort of mumble-drone. She could just make out the words – "*Hare Krishna, Hare Krishna, Krishna Krishna, Hare Hare, Hare Rama, Hare Rama, Rama Rama, Hare Hare.*"

After a few miles of stop-start congestion, horns blaring, they were unstuck from the city, out on the open, dust-blown road. Wild, heart-stopping overtaking was the norm, squeezing wary cyclists onto the scrub verge. One slow-moving vehicle appeared to be nothing but haystack. As they passed, Jane noticed it had four legs. Goats, and oxen pulling carts almost completed the arterial menagerie. Looking up, she saw vultures circling high overhead. The heat was intense, steadily increasing despite a welcome draught from the open top windows. Jane's head swam. They passed groups of weavers spinning, dyeing cloth in buckets outside white stone huts. Here and there, birds sang from trees or in flight, twittering to each other.

The bus laboured over a stream on a rustic bridge, paused for an exchange of passengers; continued. Paddy fields stretched away in all directions. Peasants toiled under the omnipresent glare, hoeing, leading cattle.

Jane turned away from the window and glanced at her companion again. Behind them, people were smoking, but she felt inhibited from lighting up. He glanced back at her, smiled uncertainly.

"You're a Hare Krishna!" she accused. "I've seen you singing and dancing, in town. On TV." He was nodding. "And one of you gave me a book once, about yoga."

"*The Perfection of Yoga*?" he enquired.

"Something like that."

"Did you like it?"

"It was interesting. I must re-read it sometime. Where are you from?"

"The spiritual world originally, but I'm based in Philadelphia, U.S.A., at the moment. And you?" He had pulled out a short loop of beads from the bag while speaking, and returned the bag to around his neck.

"Liverpool," replied Jane. "I'm on a buying expedition."

"For yourself?"

"Some things. Mainly business."

"What sort of things?"

"Oh, cloth, carvings, figures, incense." She gesticulated vaguely.

"That's nice. These things are all manifestations of Lord Krishna's material energy."

"*Who*?"

The devotee closed his eyes and rocked slightly, as if concentrating and gathering his thoughts. "*Krishna. Krishnas tu Bhagavan svyam.* Krishna is God, the supreme person, the supreme personality of Godhead. His other names include Allah, Jehovah, Buddha..."

"Christ?"

"Christ – Kristos, all the same name, but Lord Jesus was a son of god, a pure devotee."

"Oh. So what does he do?"

"As God he has nothing to do, no work, duty or *dharma*. He just enjoys the loving relationships and service of his intimate devotees. He engages in many wonderful pastimes, however. Five thousand years ago, He appeared as always, to annihilate the miscreants, deliver his devotees and re-establish the eternal principles of religion, *sanatana-dharma*."

"Annihilate who?"

"Demons. Like er.. monsters. In this age though, He appears as the *maha-mantra* to kill the demoniac mentality within us."

"So where did all this happen?"

"*Vrindavan*," replied the devotee. He looked happy, as if he had been waiting a long time to get there.

"Must be a beautiful place," remarked Jane, catching his enthusiasm.

"It certainly is. It's where Krishna tended the cows and played with the cowherd friends, enjoying his childhood pastimes."

"What did he do after that?"

"Well, it's a long story. You should really read the *Bhagavad-Gita* first."

"Go on. What happened when he grew up?"

"All right. Do you want to hear about the story of the Syamantaka jewel?"

"OK"

"Right." The devotee bowed his head and mumbled something complicated. "Well, it starts with King Satrajit, who lived near *Dvaraka*, the city Krishna reigned in when he was older. Satrajit was a great devotee of the Sun-god."

"Where's *Dvaraka*?" interrupted Jane.

"Oh, Gujarat, West India," explained the devotee. "The original city's now submerged under the Arabian Sea.

"Well, Surya, the Sun-god was so pleased with Satrajit that he gave him the fabulous Syamantaka jewel. This gem was so effulgent that when he wore it going into Dvaraka, people ran to Krishna saying the Sun-god had come to see him."

"Was Krishna fooled?"

"Naa, 'course not.

"Satrajit installed the jewel on an altar in his palace and worshipped it. It was making him... a hundred and seventy pounds of gold a day, and preventing famine and sickness anywhere in the vicinity, not that there'd be any misfortune with Krishna around, anyway."

Behind her dark sunglasses, Jane's eyes opened a degree wider.

"So Krishna asked Satrajit to give the jewel to King Ugrasena."

"I thought Satrajit was the king?"

"He was; ancient India had lots of them. Ugrasena was like the, er, ruling overlord of many dynasties, not to mention being Krishna's grandfather."

"God's grandpa?!" repeated Jane in a sneer of disbelief.

"Never mind that for the moment," he dismissed her objection. "Just remember, God can do anything he wants to. Yeah?"

She shrugged, anxious to continue the story.

"But Satrajit, being too materialistic, wanted to keep the gem for himself. So that was that. Now one day, his younger brother Prasena borrowed it to wear as he went horse riding in the forest. Unfortunately, he was killed by a lion who took the jewel away to a mountain cave. The lion, in turn, was killed by Jambavan, the gorilla king. Jambavan was a devotee of Lord Ramachandra – that's Krishna in another form – so he wasn't much into material riches, and just gave the jewel to his young son to play with.

"Meanwhile, in the city, when Presena didn't return, King Satrajit wrongly assumed that Krishna had killed him for the Syamantaka jewel, and began spreading false rumours.

"Krishna didn't like this at all, so to clear His name led a party to look for Prasena. Presently, they found his body, and that of his horse, dead; then, following a trail of gold pieces left by the jewel, they came across the lion's body. This was by the entrance to Jambavan's cave. Krishna told His companions to wait for him while he went in.

"At the end of a long tunnel, he found the Syamantaka jewel, lying next to a child. As He picked it up, the child's nurse cried out, and Jambavan reappeared, enraged.

"Because of his anger, he didn't recognise Krishna as his Lord, and began to fight Him ferociously. They fought with all kinds of weapons, then hand-to-hand, for twenty-eight days continuously. No ordinary person could do that sort of thing, of course. Jambavan was the strongest living being alive at the time, but even his strength faltered with the continuous blows of Krishna. Eventually, he understood that he was fighting God Himself, and gave up, bowing his head and praising the Supreme Lord. Krishna touched him, and like magic, all Jambavan's pain and fatigue were gone.

"After hearing Krishna explain everything, Jambavan gladly gave him the jewel, and his daughter Jambavati's hand in marriage. Then Krishna returned to Dvaraka happily. His companions had almost given up all hope of seeing Him again and were praying anxiously when He appeared with his new wife. The whole city became overjoyed, and celebrated the wedding for many days.

"Krishna summoned Satrajit before an assembly of kings, explained the whole story, and gave him back the Syamantaka jewel. Satrajit accepted the gem, but silently and with great shame and remorse. Returning home, he decided to mitigate his offences to Lord Krishna, by offering Him his daughter,

Satyabhama in marriage, together with the Syamantaka jewel.

"Sri Krishna accepted Satyabhama, who was endowed with all divine qualities, but the jewel he refused, returning it to King Satrajit."

"After all that He gave it back?"

"Yes. Krishna could see that in his heart, Satrajit actually wanted to keep the jewel – so he let him. He does that, fulfils everyone's desires eventually, be they material or spiritual. Satisfaction of material desires won't do you any good though, that's what Krishna was demonstrating in this pastime – the futility of material wealth."

"Wow. It's a far out story." She sniffled. "What about all those daughters though? Being given away like goods and chattels."

The devotee grinned. "Becoming Krishna's wife is about the greatest thing that can happen to anyone. Jambavati and Satyabhama must have achieved sublime devotion in their previous lives to even take part in Krishna's *lila*."

"His what?"

"Pastimes, activities."

"And what happened to the jewel? Where is it now?"

"Well, there is more to the story, like how there was a plot to kill Satrajit and take the jewel. It was last heard of in the hands of Akrura, Krishna's uncle, who should have passed it on to Satyabhama's son when he came of age. No ordinary man is able to keep it, that's for sure. I don't know where it is now though."

"Mmm." Jane nodded. "Do you..." She looked out of the window, and noticed that the road was turning into more of a village street. Light stone buildings were becoming packed together more closely. More people were working and walking around. "Do you think this is *Rajpur*?"

He shrugged. The bus shuddered to a halt. The driver turned round. "*Rajpur!*"

"My stop."

"Here, take this." He passed her a book as she stood up. "Would you like to make a donation?" She gave him a few coins as he made room for her to get by. "Haribol."

"Adios" she returned, stepping into the aisle, luggage-laden, disembarked. The bus moved again, crackling stones, spewing smoke and dust. It receded. They hadn't even told each other their names. Oh well, no matter.

She had been left in the village centre, the marketplace. A few other passengers, a family or two, were making tracks. They seemed to know where they were going. Jane didn't, nor did it seem to matter overmuch. She felt peaceful and happy. Hot and thirsty perhaps, but contentedly arrived.

Traders sat or crouched, cross-legged or sprawled on rugs. Their wares lay before them on silk or sacking. Wives and mothers led their charges, picking up goods to examine, bargaining, chattering. Some stalls were more ornate, their precious fruit shaded from the sun by tarpaulin or shack. There was no motor noise from the road, just the rumble of an ox-cart. Banyan trees shimmered through the heat. Where could she find a drink?

Jane realised the book was still in her hand and raised it to read the cover. '*Easy journey to other planets*' it proclaimed. "Curiouser and curiouser," she said. The birds called out to each other as they perched.

"Cuckoo – Cuckoo"

4   FLYING LESSON

Robert looked over the premises gloatingly. The old warehouse had been a snip, rent nominal, it having lain derelict for years. Lodged between a car hire depot and another disused warehouse, it, and its location were ideal. There was even more than adequate room inside for his newly acquired Transit van.

In an unnecessary but automatic look upwards, he checked his headspace. "Up" he commanded. "Confirm up. Slow, confirm slow." Below him, Duke street and the rest of the city's crumbling 'Creative Industry Quarter' gradually began to diminish. Outside, but for a black and white, smoked visor motorcycle helmet over his head, was the same as ever. Inside, now, more and more, recently, Robert himself felt radically different. He envisioned himself as some kind of channel for a much greater energy, quietly hiding inside the old Robert-body-shell. A technological messiah of the gods. He towered over the majestic sandstone of the floodlit Anglican Cathedral, Catholic lunar module, St. John's tower... The whole city spread itself in panorama, right up to the Liver Buildings, newly rebuilt dock dwellings... Wirral lights shone like atoms in an unexplored universe.

Every thousandth of a second, Robert fell. He plummeted down helplessly towards certain and imminent death. Speared, perhaps on basement railings, possibly perforating Liam and Sharon's lovingly polished XR3i Cabriolet with his head as they cruised down Hanover Street.

Every thousandth of a second, the teleporter caught him. Protected, itself, by two uninterruptable power supplies, it gently placed him back where he had been a millisecond ago. Then, according to voice command, a little further in whatever direction he wished to go.

"Hmmmmm" it whistled as it went about its careful business. Robert didn't bother fiddling with his headphones or swearing at Oliver (the Olivetti) as anyone else would have done. He simply calculated that he had overlooked the annoying side effect of causing air to vibrate around him at one kilohertz and resolved to reprogram at a higher, inaudible frequency.

Over Liverpool Bay, the Sun, large and red, spread its diffused rays wide in yet another spectacularly gorgeous sunset. It came in layers of wonder, horizontal streaks of golds, blues, azure streaked with dark clouds, changing by the minute. Something that, for some unfathomable reason, the chemical companies of Runcorn and Ellesmere Port did not claim at least partially justifiable credit for, in their promotional material proclaiming care for the environment.

Robert hoped he would be near-invisible at this twilight hour; if seen, at least anonymous in his helmet. *Careful*, he felt, should be his middle name. He had even made sure that the flying cat trials had taken place while Felix had been asleep, not relishing the concept of feline psychosis.

He politely requested a gentle spinning motion. Oliver obliged. He spun, mesmerised, gazing down, legs kicking like a toddler with its tummy tickled. What was he doing here? he wondered. What was the meaning of the rich tapestry of life, gazed on below? Most perplexing of all, with so much power and knowledge at his disposal, why would he have to get up for work just like anyone else tomorrow? He shook his head, making a complex geometrical pattern as he spiralled ever upwards.

The next day dawned, and with it, wage-slavery. Robert was a bit bleary-eyed, but not badly so. The novelty of being able to 'telecopt' would take some time to wear thin. He had stayed up late, but eventually, inevitably, his sensible streak – not tiredness – had won. He had rested.

To be woken, unnecessarily early, by the licking of his eyebrows. Seemingly, it would take very little to launch Felix into a state of enhanced unhingedness. Wearily, he arose. Remembering his maiden flight he woke up again, as it were, into full consciousness immediately, performed a short, enthusiastic tap dance in full view of Felix, *morninged*, and commuted in ecstatic trance.

*　　　*　　　*

His eyes glazed on the screen's surface, focused with such a high degree of concentration, he missed Josella's virtual figure, reflected a few feet in front of him.

She sighed. Such a waste. And more obsessively withdrawn than ever. If only she could... Sighed again, more hopelessly.

139

At last he caught sight of the reflection, and turned. "Hi Jo." He rose, and passed her before she remembered what she had been standing there for. It was sad. He returned. "Oh, could you ring for a collection this afternoon. Next day." He smiled, passed, walked – like a dog, like any ordinary... human. He spat the thought away.

The lab was moving, notionally to Nottingham for long distance trials. Precisely, he packed the fractaerial, the amplifier, the lot. It shouldn't be moved by carrier. Could go astray. Third person blame, registered claim. Neat, sweet, registered Hit.

Pottered about, anxious, waiting. Came the man in the van. Robert wouldn't have been keen to trust him with a library book. It left, with him.

Phil looked up from a book he was studying: *Strange Attractors, Chaotic Behaviour and Information Flow.* The van glided past his smoky window. Robert traipsed up, following it. It paused, indicated, turned right along Sunrise Way, vanished.

They greeted, downbeat.

"I've sent it packing."

"Where?" Phil knew what it was.

"Beeston." Outside, a few chocolate wrappers ran in windy gusts.

"Good Riddance," said Phil.

"It could be ... er ... long distance trials."

Phil sneered. "It could be a relief getting some distance between a kilowatt of five dimensional microwaves and my *bollocks*."

Robert snorted; again, started to chuckle. Phil joined in.

"Good riddance," he agreed. An adept at success, Robert had acted with outstanding flair in engineering failure. "Would you like to break the news to Colin or shall I?"

Phil sucked the air between his teeth, like a workman before giving an assessment of damage. "I reckon you could incur his full wrath, then others could come in on the post-mortem. Possibly."

"Git."

"Bad loser."

Robert gave him a hard stare then walked away.

It was probably best to present this in two or three bite-sized, steaming, stinking dollops. A not wholly negative progress report. A more negative progress report. An announcement of loss. Bereavement.

Stealthcomms could Rest In Peace.

And that was what happened. The board was Not Happy with Colin. Colin was Very Disappointed with Robert. Then the Fractaerial was discovered to have been lost in transit. Colin was Upset, and about to be Bloody Furious with Robert when Robert pointed out that, apologies not withstanding, this turned an expensive write-off into a fully recoverable insured loss. Colin felt unsure of where to vent his anger, and was subsequently Unjustifiably Rude to Josella, who had been having a bit of a hard time of it lately, and as a result had Words (later regretted) with the nice young man from accounts.

Robert felt obligated to make some show of being Pissed Off with Phil, and so on and so forth, until the waves of strained emotions spread ever outwards, eventually dissipating in the everyday jostle of countless spouses, lovers, friends, acquaintances, shop assistants and people at bus stops.

*   *   *

"So," exuded Colin, leaning back still further
into his corpulence, "How can we occupy your
teeming brain now, young Robert?"

Robert, through long practice at the art, managed to remain silent and sober at the rhetorical question while a series of impertinent and steadily more ridiculous answers presented themselves to him. He stared obliquely at the fountain beyond and outside, his thoughts nowhere and everywhere. Elsewhere. Suddenly he was aware that Colin was speaking.

"Nothing at all's got out to the wider scientific community. As far as they're concerned we're still in the dark ages."

Fascinated, Robert tuned in to what Colin was saying. His hand was turning a small polished crystal on his desk, tapping it on the mahogany. Unusual. Too small to be a paperweight.

"... very exciting developments indeed. We need someone who can design new kinds of operating systems, bridge the disciplines of hard and software. Not the actual optical structures of course, electronic analogues."

For the second time in recent months, a hundred disconnected parts of Robert's mind moved into synchronisation. "How many..? How many opto-transistors on one chip..?" he managed as it all clicked into place.

Colin moved closer, sharing the hint of a contagious grin. "One crystal."

Robert's toes were curling and uncurling inside his size tens. "How many?" he asked again, as much with his eyes as with the whisper that escaped him.

Colin saw that he was getting through. "One hundred thousand." He spoke softly and slowly, swallowed quickly and hard. "Device density should surpass that of conventional chips within a decade."

"Optical microprocessors???"

"Yes."

"Fast?"

"20 Bips"

"20 Mips? Wow!" Robert was impressed.

"No, 20 Bips" corrected Colin. "Twenty *billion* instructions per second."

Robert saw stars, felt dizzy. He felt the arm of the chair to make sure..."

"Twenty thousand million."

"I take it you're interested."

"Oh, most definitely." Just when he had begun scheming how to quietly resign.

Colin pushed a manila folder over the desk. Robert opened it, took out the papers and engrossed himself in the glossy pictures and text. His eloquence was lost in a series of impressed-teenage-boy exclamations. Colin pushed something else over. A form with dotted line.

"Eyes only. Signed out, signed in. You move to a new office tomorrow. Security rating triple A. Now I'll show you something else. "Do you know what this is?"

He could guess now. "A diamond?"

"Specially polished and cut, yes." And its electronic equivalent?"

Robert meltfloated. "A power transistor."

"Power doesn't really do it justice," explained Colin. If you could transform the entire output of the national grid into laser light, this could switch it on and off, no sweat."

"There's a few more of these files," continued Colin. "Spend your first week or two studying them. I'm putting Phil on something else. Your old team is being disbanded for the moment."

'Good' thought Robert.

The words of an old conversation with Phil came back to him, out of context:

"because information scattered all over", he had said.

"becomes less valuable".

He levitated, sensing the meeting's end, and uncharacteristically shook hands.

"Thank you," he gibbered.

Colin smiled indulgently, with the expression of a kindly uncle indulging his nephew with a gift of ten shillings for liquorice and pop. Robert withdrew, still gently gibbering.

Colin watched the office door shut, then opened his middle drawer and put his hand on a generously iced double cream bun.

5   Détente

The place Jane eventually found (after much nagging, and not a few gentle threats) was modest. In the best tradition of estate agent speak world over, it was described in glowing terms. Indeed, it could have been considered a most desirable residence for many of Delhi's street population, human or otherwise. The landlord called it a spacious workshop/garage. She would have called it a poky sweatshop/shed, and was, by far, nearer the mark. By the time Robert had inspected the lease and passed on his advice she managed to haggle the rent down to only about three times what an Indian would have paid. It had no back doors, but would just about contain the van. There was a simple square window by the side of the front doors; that would have to be washed and curtained. The doors were rickety wooden things; the walls, peeling whitewash on stone; the roof, standard issue shantytown corrugated steel.

Finally, she told Robert in a breathless rush over the radion't, there were no electricity or water supplies to worry about.

"Good," he said. "I won't worry about them, then."

Coming back to Delhi had been no fun. She was beginning to suffer again from heat exhaustion. Rajpur, experienced with culture-shock brevity, had been, without doubt, a materialisation of dreams wilder than she could have dreamt. Not material dreams – she could well have coped with a few more basic necessities – more like an atmosphere, a feeling, a consciousness beyond capture. The villagers were simple, and you could take that as you wished. They lived off the land, or not very far removed from it, in more or less the same way their families had for generations.

Jane had looked in vain for a hotel, but not for long. Radharani Patel, the matriarch of a well-to-do family (five acres, three cows and a bull), mildly shocked at her single-travelling status, had taken her in immediately, and treated her like a new daughter-in-law. They met at the market place, not long after she had alighted from the coach. Jane's lost, dazed expression and dangling arms told all.

Mrs Patel explained, in Hindi and perfect sign language, the lack of hotels, her own offered lodgings and the need for a drink and siesta in the fierce afternoon heat. Nodding, in no fit state to discuss anything, Jane surrendered to the mercy of her hostess, who had kindly picked up one of her suitcases. They walked an indeterminate distance. Her place to crash was a spot in a hut with other, more tangible daughters. She felt herself to be fading away somewhat in a wavy haze of heat.

She woke up as the sun was creeping lower, cramps in her bowels, and the smell of cooking drifting inside. A daughter showed her the latrine, another hole in the ground. Par for the course, really, south of Turin. Jane's one trip to Corfu had partially prepared her for a laid-back pace of life, but even so, not this.

Nearby, thin but athletic and fearsome looking hogs snorted their way through a mound of rotting trash. Smoke and hordes of midges flit through shafts of setting sunlight from between the nim trees. Even the damned flies seemed more relaxed than their city cousins.

They cooked meals in large woks and saucepans over a dung fire in the ground. The women sang swaying chants and chattered as Jane watched them create steaming masses of the usual rice, dhal, puris and chapattis. Twice during her stay, she traipsed the well worn path to the river for a bowl of water, struggling back the first time twenty minutes later wet, with a half-full bucket in her arms. They laughed, not too unkindly, and showed it how to carry it gracefully, on her head. Mrs Patel offered their food on a crowded altar for a few minutes before eating. Jane still thought in terms of minutes and hours, although no-one else seemed to. Leaving her watch off helped. Now and again, she glanced at the devotee's little book. Far out, these 'material and anti-material worlds'.

Early in the mornings they went for a bathe and a swim in the river. One had to keep an eye out for monkeys, on the prowl for an abandoned sari, or bracelet. Apart from that, it was great.

She made a point of visiting all the artisans she could find, making notes and buying various articles. There weren't many. It was a small place. Not much choice, but the goods were good enough, especially since they were virtually being given away.

Occasionally she heard a distant music around the village: the sound of *sitars*, *mridranga* drums, flutes. A few times she tried to follow it to the source but couldn't, and merely became confused. Perhaps the heat was doing something to her head.

The dust tracks were rough, just lines worn by man or cattle. At their sides were rice paddy and meadow, the grass sparse, the cattle tall, muscular and contemplative.

Jane spent part of one afternoon watching a boy hand weave a large white cloth, the swiftness of his movements around the loom belying his air of calm relaxation. The finished article seemed to be a tablecloth of some sort, or a child's tent. She admired as he grasped the dhoti he was wearing and pointed. He was making cool trouser-robes.

Close by stood another hut of cow dung, mud and straw, its inhabitants also busy weaving. These were saris, more finely woven.

The Sun followed her mercilessly as she ventured further out and up from Rajpur. The ground rushed down quickly; a verdant valley of fields, shimmering like a mirage. Streams swam, merging, diverging: Eden.

Out of all this way sat a painter catching rainbows. He was happy to show her his work, much of it on silk, a number of which she bought. He specialised in magical landscapes. Jane asked him if he ever painted anything else. Upon understanding, he absently put down the piece he was showing her and swept his gaze expansively, left to right, answering with a question of his own in singsong Hindi. Jane gathered the gist.

There were a few more occupations in the village. One couple made sandals and drum skins from the leather of old oxen. Another family made deities. Jane visited, and saw figures of Their Lordships Jagannatha, Balarama and Subhadra. The wizened little wood carver had a beatific look of calmness and serenity on his face. It was reflected in the images he carved, or perhaps it was the other way round. This was one of the most fascinating workshops yet. There were dozens of figures, thumb size to a few feet, lining walls of shelves. They were in various states of completion, some rude and chunky; others, with papier mâché or paint applied, smiled at her in delight, with oversized mouths and eyes, faces of black, white, yellow, and round, stumpy arms. She could definitely shift a couple of these.

"How much?" she asked, indicating a set three inches high.

"I say, to you miss, a hundred and fifty rupees" came the answer. The carver's hands never stopped moving for a moment. Without hesitating, Jane reached into her money-belt.

"And a good travelling box another fifty," he said, gesticulating with his head to a stack by her feet. She went on to buy a small wardrobe of deity clothes, doubling the cost.

*   *   *

Jane winced at the slipstream from a crazily-driven motor rickshaw, nearly putting her in the sort of travelling box that has brass handles. She was standing outside the Janpath Guest House, her abode now for the past fortnight. 'Hmm,' she mused, first Near-Death Experience of the day.

In the bag she held was a pack of blue and red patterned cotton and her sewing kit.

*   *   *

Robert paced the dungeon of Duke street apprehensively. He stroked his chin's meagre stubble, wishing he had a beard, or at least something to worry at for times like this.

He had finally pricked up the courage to get inoculated, and was now protected against typhoid, yellow fever, and a whole host of other horribly alien diseases.

Somehow, the fractaerial and associated equipment had materialised in a room upstairs he referred to as the control centre.

A most elaborate intruder alarm of his own design was primed to whisk away all contents of the warehouse at the slightest breach of security. He was rather proud of that. It was, by nature, unique. Anyone else with a teleport could just whip the whole building away.

"Bip! Bip!" squeaked the radion't in his back pocket. He took it out and flipped the lid open. This mark two version was a neat replica of Captain James T. Kirk's starship communicator. He had regretfully decided against disco lights in the floor, large theatrical levers and rising pitch trilling noises, however, on grounds of taste and cost.

"Hi Rob," said Jane. "I've just put the curtains up. "All ready your end?"

"Only for the past month," he remarked pleasantly.

"Well, come on then!"

"Right, let's go."

"Which way?"

"Oh, I'll be the guinea pig, don't worry. Here goes. Teleport to Delhiport, confirm, teleport to Delhiport. Jump, confirm Jump."

There was a sound like a very brief blast of an aircraft's jet engine played backwards as Robert simultaneously vanished and rematerialised. He blinked his eyes open. "My goodness, Toto, I don't think we're in Kansas anymore." He put his hands up on his temples. He already knew it worked, of course, but having it work on him was different.

"Checking your head's still there?" asked Jane.

"Are you?"

"Still here. Yes. Don't worry. You aren't lost in another dimension hallucinating."

The heatwave hit him. "No, I'm not. Do you want a go?"

"In a minute. I'll show you round the block first. Make sure you don't f-f-f-fade away."

"Ah!" He examined the telepad's interior appreciatively. Jane rattled the door open and pulled him out. He stood, swaying, agog at the Indians in white cloth, busying themselves up and down the street. A herd of goats came their way. He edged back. Jane led him around the neighbourhood, not really needing to point out points of interest, for it was all most interesting. A ramshackle district of shacks and rams – both goaty and musical, some people sat or trudged, kneading rosaries – "Rama Rama Hare Rama" they mumbled.

"There's a Rama temple over there." explained Jane, gesturing at a beautifully ornate but ramshackle old building. Actually Robert didn't find this much of an explanation.

"'I see', said the blind man, who didn't see at all, and to whom a nod was as good as a wink," he replied mysteriously. Beads of sweat ran down his face, and dark patches appeared at the armpits of his shirt. "Very lively, isn't it?" he ventured at last.

"Mmm."

They walked a bit further, ignoring the ever-present hustlers and beggars pestering them, glancing at wares for sale, refusing various proffered articles, turning corners. Robert admired the goods quietly to Jane. Soon they were back at the telepad. Jane proudly displayed her stash of stuff.

"Amazing. OK, let's ...

"Go back!"

"Go on then. You tell it. We'll go back together."

"I don't know what to say."

"Just tell it. Twice."

They stood, apprehensive, with the canvas bags around them on the floor, inside a transit-sized rectangle of chalk. Thankfully, he had dissuaded her from doing a pentacle.

"Teleport Liverpool, confirm teleport Liverpool. Jump confirm jump."

"Tzzzuuup." And they were there. Jane kept her eyes open. And to her it had not seemed such an instant thing at all. She had leapt out into a cosmic rainbow of energy. Flashes and stars of sound, the sense of falling and being driven upwards at the same time. She floundered, swaying, mouth opening and closing like a fish, and sat down on the cold floor.

Outside was murky and squalid and familiar. He chucked the Transit's keys at her. "Home, Jane." She climbed aboard. It was a comfortably rusty blue, with yellow roof, the sort of vehicle no self respecting cowboy builder or fruit and veg trader would be without. They took the scenic route down Princes Avenue back to her place and unpacked. The flat seemed musty, dusty, neglected. She shivered a lot, even inside a newly donned mohair jumper, wrinkled her nose at the pile of bills and junk mail, and put them all down on a square inch of table not occupied by spell books, crystals, tarot cards and string.

Robert made some coffee, then got his laptop computer out and started punching away at it. She found some old tobacco and made a revoltingly dry rollie.

"Look, let me tidy up and have a snooze then we could go out later for a meal. Work out what to do next."

"OK," he said, hardly looking up. "The Mahabarat at 8?"

"Where's that?"

"Mahatma Ghandi Street."

"Oh. Greenwich Mean Time?"

"Uh, tell you what, ring me when you wake, and I'll pick you up then."

That sounded simple enough. Of course Robert ended up ringing her, as she overslept, then she had to get up, then it took five and a half hours as the watch flies to get back to Delhi. They ate, very late, at a window table. The van, parked outside, seemed highly incongruous.

"Lakshmi" retorted Jane. "Lakshmi trading."

"Transform Trading."

"Lakshmi is the goddess of fortune. Can't go bust with a name like that.

"We travel by Fourier Transform. Going bust is the least of our worries." He chewed another mouthful of vindaloo deliberately. Jane had warned him to go easy on the food at first. He was ignoring her. "Can't really go wrong with technology like this."

"Who's going to be going round selling it all?"

"Who's paying for it?"

"Who's got cancer of the ego?"

He pulled a snarl at her and capitulated. Delhi was more or less closing down by the time they finished, so they got a taxi to Birkenhead, where it was not yet midnight, went to an awful nightclub and got horribly drunk.

6   ALTRUISM AND ADVENTURE

Somehow they managed to sort out the paperwork so Lakshmi looked legitimate. Robert's diarrhoea subsided. Jane returned to England by plane with 'something to declare'. They sorted out registration and insurance for 'another', 'identical' van in Delhi, advertised a wholesale fruit & veg delivery service, and soon Jane was frantically bombing around with crates of fresh exotic delicacies to all the best shops and restaurants in a twenty mile radius. She was careful to buy local, too, and managed a few five a.m. expeditions a week to Edge Lane wholesale market, for appearance's sake. Dave got the pick of the bunch. She was still sentimental about him, and he was quite good at buying the other stuff. 'Hippie paraphernalia' as Robert called it. Tuesday afternoons were usually sufficient for unloading cloth, clothes, jewellery, knick-knacks and incense at Quiggin's warehouse of stalls in town, and the rest went on occasional Sunday mornings at Waterloo Dock market.

Within two months, their biggest problem was concealing sizeable quantities of cash. Jane acquired an attractive tan, and a reputation amongst her friends, unbeknown to Robert, for having an ever-fresh supply of top quality hash and sensomelia. Her flat became a repository for exotic rugs, carpets and pictures. She managed to avoid the lure of stronger psychedelics. Dave dropped in on one night's party and was most affable. Even Robert seemed to be more at peace with himself, lulled from acute paranoia by the non-appearance of robed assassins at his door.

They took a few brief vacations to the world's beauty spots – Antarctica, the South Sea Islands, the Caribbean, Venice, Tibet, China, California, and what remained of the Brazilian rain forests. The machine landed them at night, and a few times more, Jane felt a twinge of that feeling the first time she teleported.

One night, they went for an Indonesian meal in Bangkok after Robert read the virtues of that land's cooking in his Sunday Times. He was trying out a more efficient version of the travel-transfer software. They ate and ate, but for several days felt tired and hungry, however much they consumed. Eventually he tracked down the bug to an exclusive-OR subroutine which had performed a left-right reflective transformation on the molecules of their body cells, making normal food indigestible.

"Robert," spoke Jane one day as they pottered about the Duke Street telepad, "This is all very well, but what about saving the world?"

"What about it? How about buying an island nature reserve off South Africa or something?"

"Fascist! How can you be so, so, Unaware! Unless the idea is to put all the crazy heads of government on it?"

"What's wrong with developing the business a bit? Becoming the richest, most powerful family on earth?"

She looked into his eyes, and didn't like what she saw. Not at all.

"We could licence little taps beamed an endless supply of fizzy mineral water, for an annual subscription."

"And you think that'll make mankind happier!?!" she shouted. "You've got about as much idea as a ..."

"No, it'll just make us a lot of money."

"Piggy money box!" she finished. "Can't you think beyond your own belly?"

"How about cars powered by the sun's energy? Telebeamed straight into the power unit? They'd be extremely popular."

"Maybe. How about beaming food to the starving, or nuclear waste into outer space. That would be even more popular."

"Maybe. But who would buy it?"

"Robert!!!" Even he could see he had gone too far, tried to pacify her.

"OK, even IBM gives to charity. It's good for public relations I suppose, if we ever have any. There's no reason why we can't do good as well. How about getting rid of some nuclear waste.?"

"Right on, matey! That'll benefit the Earth for thousands of years. Just beam it all away."

"I think we should do some exploratory tests first, Jane. It's a massive undertaking."

"Like what?"

"Get our space legs. Investigate the cosmos first hand before we start filling it up with nuclear pooh."

"And missiles."

"I'd have thought you'd include them under pooh, myself."

"I would indeed. Shall we go?"

"Be my guest. I fancy a space suit myself. Been considering acquiring one for a while, actually."

"What, like a deep sea diving suit?"

"I was thinking more of the genuine article."

"How could...?"

"NASA exhibition centre, Cape Canaveral."

"That's theft. We could just borrow them, I suppose."

* * *

The joystick wriggled under his finger. Jane sat at his side in the other swivel chair shouting instructions. The screen showed a dark, infra-red telescan of NASA's Florida visitor centre. Their camera was fly-hovering through the exhibition.

Apollo antiques lay scattered all around on futuristic-looking pedestals. Befitting its subject, the place was huge. They passed a hundred mementoes of Kennedy's dream – cratered command capsule, moon rocks ("Are you sure you haven't been here before?" asked Jane), photographs and holograms, booster and landing rockets.

The camera passed a gargantuan fibreglass moon segment, flowed on, then jerked back to a group of dummies.

"Waxworks," said Robert. "In priceless togs. How tall are you?" The figures stood proud, hands raised in greeting, some, frozen, stepping forward.

"Five-five." A red line moved over the screen, darting from suit to suit, stretching and shrinking. Digits at the bottom right span up and down.

"Gotcha!" He snapped the fire button. And it was gone. They heard a crashing noise behind them and turned. John Glenn lay overbalanced, eyes open, on the floor.

Jane whistled. "Immense."

"Crucial!" agreed Robert, popping another suited dummy. It fell behind the first.

"Yeah, We've got them!" she cried. "I'm all excited now. Let's have a look at Sellafield while the camera's hooked up."

"OK. Watch," he inflected dryly, flicking a rollerball. The scene diminished as the camera rose high. Evidently night vision was poor from this height; a sort of plan took over. Florida flowed into central America. Coastline scrolled away to the left. Europe and the Mediterranean rolled on from the right. Gradually the screen homed in on Great Britain, Northwest, Cumbria: Sellafield. She squirmed in her seat. The TV picture reappeared. Dawn was breaking. A sprawl of utilitarian buildings and plant became visible and slowly grew.

"There's some." He pointed to an area of pools. Dim blue light seeped out from beneath the surface of one. "That's the hottest".

The camera homed in on it, larger, closer and closer.

"It's evil. Get a fix on it Rob. Blast it off to the Sun. Or Pluto."

"That's just what I'm doing," he explained slowly, almost kindly, as if to an ignoramus. Jane glared at the pool angrily. Water vapour steamed off it in gusts. Below the surface they could make out some sort of outline.

"Stacked fuel rods. They leave them here to cool off for years, don't they."

"Yeah. Bastards." The shapes had an eerie glow about them.

"Their blueness makes them look cold, not hot at all."

"Hmm. Don't they just. I could put a Geiger counter on the camera for this sort of thing."

"Can it go underwater?"

"Not at the moment. Actually it's going to pick up an unpleasant dose of radiation as it is. Even this far away."

The screen missed a beat. A black line rose up to the top. Beneath it was a mess of snow-noise.

"Shhhh*it*!" Robert exclaimed.

"What's happened?"

He hit a few keys, read the display on the other monitor. "We've lost it." He spun in his chair. "Camera failure. Must be the radiation. We've still got it at Duke Street but... it must be hot as hell. Damn!"

"Ah well, let's blast it."

"No. Mission aborted."

"Oh come on! You got a fix, didn't you?"

"I'm not messing about with anything as dangerous as this with half of the equipment out of order."

"Robert!" she shouted. "Don't you want to save the world?"

He shrugged. "Tell you what. We'll check out the suits tomorrow. Maybe go somewhere."

"Huh!" Jane left in a huff. Robert reached for the TV camera technical manual and leafed through it, grimacing in sympathy with the Transit's gear box as she revved up and squealed off outside.

The next day after work, they tried the suits on, which were moderately uncomfortable. With the big round helmet clamped on Jane felt like blowing a raspberry at Robert, but then realised she might have to put up with a splattered visor for some time. He had been quick about fitting radion'ts, anyway.

NASA were being cagey about their loss. No news reports he was aware of had been released. Had the CIA and the President been informed? Would they suspect anything? Probably nothing more than a few employees. Ha! Morons.

It was twilight by the time they were ready. The suits' oxygen and safety indicators were fine. Only one thing remained – to fly.

"Let's go!" urged Jane. The only thing missing was some inspiring music. Her heartbeat and their shared breathlessness made do.

"Where to, baby Jane? We can go... anywhere, ... anywhere at all." Robert felt remote, detached, amused.

"Alpha Centuri. Let's fly there at the speed of light. See if there's another Earth."

"That'll take four years. Approximately."

"Oh, we can speed up later. I don't want to just *arrive*. I want to travel through space."

"Amen to that. OK, ready?" They both were, having been to the loo in preparation for a long, distant journey.

"Yeah."

"Teleport vector Alpha Centuri, speed C, confirm teleport Alpha Centuri speed C. Jump, confirm Jump."

And with a flash, they vanished.

*   *   *

All the colour was gone from their faces,
all expression, save shock, which in its acute
form is perhaps just an absence of same.

"Who ... " they asked each other "the hell is that?!?" – speechless for an answer. Jane's mind was numb; Robert's brain raced: neither could work out anything to do but what the man asked. Jane clanked off into the spare room to disrobe.

Back in civvies, she followed Robert down the stairs. The man was sitting at the kitchen bench with a steaming pot of coffee and a bowl of pistachio nuts. He had taken his coat off and hung it over the end of the stairs, poured himself a mug, and was busily engaged in peeling the nuts, tossing them into a wide open mouth and masticating.

"Do sit down," he indicated between mouthfuls.

Robert half-expected to be invited to make himself at home, so at ease was this visitor – intruder (?). They sat round the pine table in the middle of the room, surrounded by neat white appliances. Felix appeared, jumped up to a window-ledge, rubbed against the glass, and gave his plaintive silent miaow to be let in. He was ignored.

"My name... You may call me Alistair. Alistair Magee. I represent..." Maddeningly, he stopped to pour their beverages. "Milk? Sugar?"

They took, grateful at least for something to do with their hands. Jane removed a packet of Silk Cut from her jacket and lit up, automatically.

"Nuts? No, perhaps not." He fished ineffectively in his teeth with a finger to dislodge a particularly stubborn pistachio particle and continued. "I represent a... group, an organisation err... interested in your invention, Mr Ashley."

So, this was it. Robert watched Magee's hands closely. When would the gun come out? What next?

"We already have the ability to... as you can see." He smugged. "I have been authorised to offer you an enhanced telekinetic ability." He blinked and leaned back. "Both of you." They waited, for "the price being, of course, the technology in your possession."

He carefully avoided saying 'your technology,' noted Robert. In fact, he seemed to know a hell of a lot. Robert swivelled a glance at Jane suspiciously. "What if I say no?"

Magee unclasped his hands and took a small electronic game from a jacket pocket. He unhinged it and began to play, to the accompaniment of a series of annoying bleeps. Finally it gave out a tinny sort of explosive noise. "Annihilation," he said, leaving open the possibility that he was in communication with still darker forces. "You have not been betrayed." He motioned at Jane. "In fact, you have been extremely clever. We have been disturbed by your use of pi- and mu-level realities."

"The fourth and fifth dimensions?"

"Yes."

"Which you use without recourse to technology?"

"Of a sort... more commonly referred to as mystic siddhis."

"You don't look like a yogi to me" said Jane. "Who are you?"

Magee stared at her as he cracked another pistachio and tossed it into his gaping mouth. "A senior member of an ancient world-wide organisation dedicated to" crunch, crunch, "the enlightenment and evolution of humanity."

"And the self-interest of its members," added Robert.

"And you're being offered membership! We need people like you."

"Thank you," said Robert. "I'm sure you do."

"What are you called?" asked Jane.

"We have a symbol."

"What is it?"

"The eye in the pyramid."

"Illuminati," spoke Robert.

"Illuminati?" chorused Jane.

"Yes."

"You're being very candid aren't you?" asked Robert. "For a secret society?"

"You're very special... initiates," explained Magee.

"What does membership involve?" he asked.

"I'm glad you asked that. Intensive training and, considering your present situations, new identities."

"New what?" asked Jane, considerably perturbed.

Magee raised his eyes to Heaven.

"So what have you been up to all these years?"

He chuckled. "Like our old friends! Ha!, Oh, behind the scenes control and manipulation of world events. A little commerce. The odd, assassination. *Atlantis, Dwarka*, Egypt, Greece, the rise and fall of this, that and the other."

"For what purpose?"

"I've already told you."

"And what else?"

"You'll find out in the course of your instruction."

"We're in," said Robert flatly. To Jane, "OK?"

"OK, although I do seem to have some deep philosophical reservations."

"As long as they're not for tickets to destruction, I'll take that as an affirmative. We'll transport the contents of your premises to Boot Camp straight away."

Open mouthed, they vanished again.

7   BREAKFAST AT INGOLSTADT

A low droning like planes overhead – but from below – sounded. Very deep below, very deep. Plenty of power there. A sound that seemed to ... change somehow ... the more closely he listened to it.

Robert stirred and lifted himself up on one elbow. He was lying under a puffy blue duvet on golden silk sheets. He leant on one matching blue pillow as he stretched to take in his surroundings. The room was huge and ridiculously opulent. Platinum bed and fittings, oak panelling, Turkish *Hereke* carpet, with en-suite shower and dressing areas. No windows though, not so much as a peephole.

A polite double knock disturbed his contemplation. The floor to ceiling pine-inlaid-with-ivory doors swept open to admit a visitor.

"Cuthbert Jennings, at your service" announced the swarthy youth before him. "The time is eight a.m. Breakfast will be served at nine. I have some letters awaiting your signature."

From the waist up he was dressed as an eighteenth century valet, with frilly white shirt, cravat and black buttoned tunic. Below, he had on a pair of Levi 501s with a large silver skull buckled belt and oversized technicolor trainers, looking more like a 23rd century architectural monstrosity than mere footgear. He plumped a pink briefcase down on the bed. "The combination is all fives. Please ring if you have any need of assistance."

Robert noticed a bell push on the wall above his head

"Goodbye."

Robert reclined and opened the briefcase. It contained a silver Waterman fountain pen, and a few pages of A4. They were neatly typed to his bank, employer, building society and doctor. He had apparently left for an unspecified destination, c/o a disreputable firm of solicitors on Dale Street. It seemed remarkably straightforward for such a supposedly subterfugic and conspiratorial organisation. He unclipped the pen and washed his hands of the documents with resignation.

What he knew of their design was sketchy, and came from the most dubious of sources – a treacle like trilogy of subterfuge and subplot, chaotic, rambling, barely readable drivel lent to him by Phil.

Ohhh! He put his head in his hands. No! It couldn't be true. One of the authors, in a slightly more lucid sequel, or apology, had admitted it to be so. Had complained in fact, of nuts ringing him up pretending to be involved. This wasn't happening.

The chandelier gleamed in defiance. It hung there, dangling from the hand-carved plaster ceiling, providing employment for a bevy of finest white ten-carat diamonds. He ducked undercover for a moment, clenched his teeth and came back out.

"Arggh" he moaned, throwing back the rest of the duvet. He would just have to deal with it as best he could. After all, things could be worse. Showered and shaved, he dressed in a comfortable and smart set of designer-label jeans, shirt and jacket from one of the built-in wardrobes and consulted his new Rolex Oyster Perpetual. Five to already. Breakfast time.

He rang the bell. Jennings re-entered and gave a half-sneer.

"Here you are. I've signed the letters."

Jennings took the briefcase. "Thank you sir. May I show you to the dining room?"

"By all means," assented Robert, who had no idea how else he was going to get there.

They glided down a wide and light passageway, lit by source unseen.

"Here," indicated Jennings, pushing open a set of identically ostentatious doors.

Robert entered, followed by the valet. A glass table in the room's centre was set for breakfast. Around its circumference sat Magee, Jane, and two other young women. At least this room had some style, thought Robert. The far end, on his right, was open to one of the most spectacular views he had ever seen. Snow-capped mountains, glacier runs, purples, pinks, whites and oranges assaulting his sense of sight. It must have been a window though. Here and there, a flurry of snow hit it and fell. In it, he could see a reflection of the log fire, set in a stone pillar fireplace. The room's walls were likewise, bare stone, the floor deeply carpeted.

"Hi Rob," said Jane. "This is Caroline..."

"Hi," said Caroline, rising. "Caroline Steinbeck, pleased to meet you, Robert." She sat down. She was tanned, with black hair and a strong New York accent.

"and Ananda..."

"Hello Robert."

Her voice, her sculptured face, in fact her entire self was obviously Deutsche. "Ananda Pris."

She wore a cleanly tailored white shirt with black jeans, and stood nearly as tall as him. "I am your siddhi coach. Please sit down."

He drew up a chair and sat.

"Hello Rob," said Magee. "That's all the introductions done then. Welcome to Ingolstadt."

"Where?" asked Robert.

"Ingolstadt," repeated Magee. "International Solar System headquarters. Central admin., training." He waved his hands about a bit as if that would cover all other eventualities.

"We're in the side of a mountain," explained Jane. "In Tibet."

"Tea or coffee?" enquired Cuthbert Jennings.

"Coffee," replied Robert. "If it hasn't been doped."

"Milk?"

"Yes."

Jennings poured a cup carefully, added a little milk, raised it to his own lips, drank a good gulpful, then splattered it out over the floor.

"I'm rather afraid it has." He put the remains of the cup down sharply on Robert's saucer. Caroline and then Magee began to smirk.

Robert and Jane looked at each other seriously. Jane swallowed. "Bread roll?" she offered. He took the nearest, trying to examine it surreptitiously for a hidden message.

The rest of breakfast consisted of tomato soup and a Greek salad.

"Nice property," understated Robert.

"Thanks," said Magee. "It does."

"Do many people live here?" asked Jane.

"Just us," replied Caroline.

"Who built it?"

Caroline looked around. "Some of it's ancient. Natural rock formation. We just extended it as required, didn't we?"

"You mean you teleported chunks of rock out of the inside of the mountain to make rooms?"

"Yeah. Why shouldn't we? Stuff like that can be a bit draining though. That's where your machine'll come in handy, won't it?"

"OK. It will. Now what? Alistair mentioned something about giving us initiation, mystic powers." Jane dabbed at her mouth with a napkin and pushed her plate away.

Ananda glanced at them both alternately, and spoke, in her precise, guttural manner. "If you believe you are up to it, yes. I can take you there. Alternatively, something more... easier can be arranged."

Robert finished his last cube of fetta cheese, the one he had been keeping as an end-morsel. He met Jane's eyes, then Ananda's. "Take us there."

"OK." She snapped her fingers. "Sofa."

A portion of the carpeted floor split and slowly moved apart to allow a great black leather sofa to rise out and up, facing the window. Ananda walked over to it briskly.

"Sit. Plees."

They followed. Sat. Relaxed and lay a little further into it. Jane turned her head and peered up to watch Magee and Caroline leave. Cuthbert Jennings was already gone.

Ananda stood to their left, slightly forward, allowing them a full view of the mountains. Jane put out a hand on the sofa between them.

Robert placed one on top. "What's your room like?"

"All sheets and cushions. Lots of stuff from the flat, lots of new stuff. Yin-yangs. Omms. It's cool. And yours?"

"Oh, it's like the penthouse suite at the Ritz. Bit overdone. Very nice" he added, aware of Ms Pris standing beside them.

She began: "To give you the powers without knowledge would be unwise. I am going to give you the initial part of the illumination. Later we may do some exercises. Look out now. What do you see?"

"Mountains"

"A glacier"

"Snow"

"Clouds"

"Look at the glacier. Here." She pointed. They nodded and stared. Like a serpent, it slid down between rocks the size of houses, scraping its way through a giant crevasse, rainbows shining through the snow, lying, packed on its surface.

Robert felt the humming below. It was changing pitch. Rising, almost imperceptibly.

8 Glacier Trip

"The modern Bavarian Illuminati was 'founded' by Adam Weishaupt, a professor of cannon law and former Jesuit, at Ingolstadt in 1776. You may have heard that before. The organisation dates back a lot further than that of course; very much further."

The glacier began to shimmer. It was growing, began to move, with – more speed than a glacier should, like there was going to be an avalanche; suddenly expanded to fill her whole vision. She took a great inward breath; was travelling down its path, as it grew, into a river, gliding, speeding as it stretched down the valley.

"Back to the source, a long way I assure you, a hidden place, like the Ganges, with its origins far beyond this world."

She was flying like a jet; could feel the acceleration as she banked and turned; heart in mouth she twisted to look beside her. No-one, nor rush of air, just the sound of Ananda's crisp, teutonic commentary. The land was a blur; down she hurtled with it, faster still.

"We go right back now, to an earlier age."

Suddenly, she hit the sea, could sense the smack of an abrupt change in density; the light dimmed; aquamarine shadows flit past – schools of fish, dolphins, whales? What if she hit one at this speed?

Just as the light had almost extinguished to an inky blackness, it began to grow again, with another quality: magical, etherial.

"The last truly high civilisation on this planet. A place of riches beyond dreams. Pleasure gardens, fantastic temples and palaces, great schools of philosophy..."

Dawn was rising, and now she (they?) seemed to be flying, slowing, high, but descending, over plains of corn and rape. Here and there, houses of unusual structure and colour grouped themselves. Hills, streams and forests passed below. Presently she *arrived* at the walls of a large city, rising at an angle. Looking to the left and right, Jane saw triangular peaks. She surmised the city plan was square, with a pyramid at each corner. High into their golden sides four great eyes stared out.

"Guardians of Horus. They watched without, and each other, not knowing that seeds of destruction lay deep within. The pyramid's designers received their skill and knowledge from extra-terrestrial sources, and consequently guarded their secrets closely. They became known to themselves as the Brotherhood, were the first great master stone-masons, and used hyrographs as secret symbols depicting tools of their trade like the spread compass. Initiation was difficult, often painful or degrading, and involved many levels. The neophyte would be quite unaware of the number, aims and practices of levels beyond his own."

Now inside the walls, she glided over beautifully ornamented residential quarters, tree lined avenues, areas of commerce and work, shops, the buildings growing steadily larger, grander, more exquisite in their detail.

"The Brotherhood represented a fourth centre of power, balancing and playing off priesthood, scribes and government – the king and his ministers. The power structures worked closely together; the Brotherhood, however, being a secret society beyond its most rudimentary levels, and having high-placed members in the government and priesthood..."

"ran the whole show," finished Jane.

"Precisely," said Pris.

She was approaching the city centre, a vast concourse, with trees and flowered borders surrounding the highest pyramid of them all. Past that, to her left, stood a majestic palace. It seemed to be made of white marble. Trellises and balconies swept up to it. They did not turn, but stopped in front of the pyramid.

"The culture was known as that of Mummu. The remnants of its priestly class later became known as the Justified Ancients of Mu, or the JAMs. They were actually allied with us for some thousands of years – we absorbed them as an offshoot of a lower initiatory level but then..."

Gradually, Jane became aware that the pyramid had started to pulse at a slow rate. The sound was low and powerful. She tried to place it, for it had a tinge of familiarity, but could not. It was glowing with a soft effulgence, sort of yellow white, then darkening, in time with the sound. They started to move again, closer and closer. The edifice was closing in on her; she was heading straight for the centre of the great eye, still high above the ground. Nearer still, Jane heard herself cry out, then was upon its pulsing, heaving, humming surface.

She passed through the iris at the peak of illumination; it seemed to suck her to it with a great inward breath.

"Oh God!" murmured Robert.

She had almost forgotten about him. All she could see was row upon row of white-robed figures prostrating themselves before a smaller version of the pyramid they were now inside. A circular wall of light-coloured stone enclosed the space, which was large, but not of cathedral proportions. Simple, stark pillars glowed with a cool blue light, supporting a ceiling at most a few stories high.

"Are you there? Are you OK?" she asked.

"Yeah"

"Our later program with the Pharaohs of Egypt had to be conducted on a much more basic level. There, the rejuvenating powers of the pyramid to concentrate energies were merely, or ostensibly, used to preserve the dead. Or perhaps we were just becoming more discreet by then." She left the question open. "What you see here..."

Again the pyramid was central, priests arranged around it in four-block squares, one to each side. En masse, seemingly without signal, they raised themselves to a sitting posture. Each crossed his legs under him in what Jane recognised as full lotus position. Every one of them was sitting on a small furskin mat. They placed their hands gently on their knees, palms upward, forefingers and thumbs touching, open in a circle.

"... is a meditation on form." The sound dipped lower for a moment, filling her frame with its deep, intense vibration. She shuddered. Then, gradually, it began to rise. The figures were motionless, their eyes fixed, boring into the pyramid within a pyramid. It seemed to come from no particular direction, rather from within, in the same way that there was no smell at all, and, had she thought about it, neither hot, cold nor warm sensations. It was strengthening, not pulsing any more, steady, inescapable, all encompassing. The pyramid stared at her stonily. She was drawn to it. Now there was a warmth. The eye was its source. It glowed a dark, terrible crimson, changing, lightening at the top to a bright scarlet. The redness melted downwards. Its tip became fiery orange, spreading towards the base.

'Oh God, it's alive,' she thought. 'It's alive. It's going to get me and I don't care!'

A bright yellow shone from the tip as the sound swept up further in pitch. Changing faster. The molten light glistened larger, fuller, sweeping away all thoughts of otherness. Nothing else but this. Yellow merged to light green. Everything always leading up to – emerald, seeping down – this moment, it had all been a dream. Only this was real, would ever be; would all else stop now I've found... Could feel it dripping *down her*. She probed it. Eye ris. A dot in a fish, a tennis bat. Eyelash aerofoil. Sweeping curly legs on a table, staring back, the round cloth hanging, underwater, in the air; sky swept blueness, sing that pure sweet tone in my ears, my eyes, *whose* eyes? My heart. My heart. My heart. Three eyes, onedigo hanging skittles. Will burst, with love, boundless love at the end, high humming too soft, beat louder my child, my friend. Rise past ears' threshold, take hold of my mind. To velvet violet, crescendo of peaks, to the end of the rainbow. Let my love leap!

ANGELS CHÎC

*   *   *

Floated in ecstasy, more like... Like what? Like...
no more words, just light, and light, just blissness.
Coming and crying and coming and crying.

_9_   MOON GODDESS

The humming, throbbing, underground sound had risen in pitch and melodiousness. It now resembled a ghostly, or heavenly choir. Its voices' notes could not quite be picked out, but, the effect was quite, no – more than – pleasant.

He walked – or was it more like dancing? – on a fluffy light surface. Whatever, it seemed to take care of itself. The tall arches and columns were a breathtaking blend of something like Greek, Neo-Georgian, Roman; the scale, gargantuan, the furniture, chic. Glasses of slightly coloured drinks proffered themselves on ledges all around. He took an orange one, sniffed, sipped, then gulped. It was delicious. Not noticeably alcoholic, tasting nothing like any beverage he knew. He replaced the drained glass. Far away, other people were milling, like silhouettes in the mist. He gravitated in their direction, draining a few more cocktails as he went.

Everything glowed with a warm, clean brilliance, in soft pastel shades of off-white. A shining blue sphere caught his eye. It was bouncing along in very slow motion, illuminating the vicinity with a soft, pastel hue. There was another, more intense, the size of a golf ball in soft yellow. It collided with the blue beach ball-sized globe, deforming it. It re-formed; they scattered, knocked off course towards a different pocket of this world. The whole place was similarly illuminated, in a delightful arrangement. It was like the effect of a hundred misty sunrises and sunsets mixing simultaneously.

A cat sprang across his path, its coat a whirl of oranges, pinks, greens, and magentas. Following it, a trio of psychedelically patterned kittens, one with two heads, bounded and flew. Robert stopped and shook his head slowly, as if watching the women's final at Wimbledon or preparing to cross the road. He looked up. The pillars were so high... A shooting star scorched its parabolic trail. The few brighter stars and planets twinkled. One of them was huge, obscuring half the sky. And blue. Twilight. Outside.

He began to frown, but his face couldn't manage it. Everything was perfect. Starting off again, he passed clumps of apple and banana trees, swaying in a breeze so soft it might have been nothing more than breath. Fantastic flowers, like creations from the Magic Roundabout, stood prettily, sprouting and trailing from the ledges. He inhaled their aroma deeply, growing yet more blissful. Some ledges contained cool, clear liquids, like fonts, or baths, at different levels. He leant over one. His face loomed up, looking almost as it had in his youth, but more handsome; it lacked the acne. An eye in pyramid motif was tattooed low and centrally on his forehead. He dipped his face and hands in, splashing icy droplets, and withdrew, watching the expanding circles of waves distort his reflection.

Turning round, he saw a bouncing red globe, shining through a fountain, spreading shadow stripes over the milky leaves of a luxuriant rose bush beside him. The stripes took off, fading as they grew longer. He continued, becoming aware of an intricate bird song. It mingled harmoniously with a soft, reverberating beat as he approached the gathering's outer edges.

People were dressed as if for some bizarre futuristic fashion show. No-one seemed much older than himself. They took little notice of him. He looked down. His own attire was just like theirs. Tiredness was hard to imagine.

Compulsively, he joined in the dancing, copying their movements. The company was mixed. Several times he thought he would drop at the sight of a few of the dancing goddess-girls.

One, in silk silver cling-pants and a fishnet top over her sheer black brassière, stared back at him brazenly. Her hair was blonde, plaited into a rearward-pointing cone. Around her neck was a small, colourful flower garland. Wilfully she smiled.

"Hi" he tried to say, but other sounds came out. "Hi. Where am I?"

Her smirk opened to reveal straight white teeth and a darting tongue. "Where am I?" she sang, in mocking repetition. "What planet are you from?"

"Me? I'm from Earth."

"Ah." She looked up, continuing with her pointy, dancing movements, moving her flowing fingertips to indicate his forehead. "Illuminati Primus. Your first trip."

"Yup." He repeated the question.

"They can be a bit unhelpful to new initiates, can't they? Never tell them where they're going, what they're supposed to be doing..."

"Why?"

"Why?"

"Why I'm here, or... if it really matters." His expression changed again from puzzlement to relief. He was having a damn good time. The place was full of cool chics. Who cared where he was?

"Sure it matters," she replied, taking his hand, leading him back and forth in a graceful two-step. "Have you no idea really?"

"No."

"It takes colossal sacrifice to send a person here from the middle planets. It is not done lightly. Or easily," she added, continuing her pointy finger-dancing.

"Here?"

"Chandraloka; what you know, or rather have no idea of, as the moon. The land of Vibhavari, the capital, and court of King Amritamaya. It corresponds on your more gross physical maps with Mount Serao on the Sinus Aestuum plain."

"Oh" he replied. "It's like heaven, isn't it?"

"It is heaven."

"Ah. I should have known that something like this was going to happen when the pyramid exploded."

She nodded. "Still using that old Mu-an sacrifice, huh?"

"Am I dead?"

She moved her head to one side and frowned as if puzzled. Suddenly her arm jerked, pulling him towards her, mouth open, tongue twisting inside his cheeks.

They disengaged. He let his heartbeat slow before speaking.

"Sorry. That was a stupid question. Look, I'm Rob, although I don't usually look like this."

"You're used to a more gross body. Right? I'm Parija."

He felt his hand move to shake in a reflex action, then checked it.

"Let's go then. You want to slow down, get your bearings. I need to stop dancing. I've been here years." She pulled, he followed.

'Years?' What had she been doing? Waiting for him? The phrase triggered something in his subconscious. Something about time. What was it?

"Years?" he repeated.

"Yeah. Mind you, time is only relative."

Forget it. He couldn't handle much right now. Things were a little spacey as they were, without having to think about them too deeply.

They boarded a swan. The creature had been sitting, drifting, in a small pond, admiring its reflection. As they stepped on to the feather lined seat, it lifted its head and spread a huge pair of wings. Smoothly it arose. They were aloft. Robert heard Parija speak softly to the bird, words, or swanspeak he couldn't make out.

If he'd had imagination, this would have been one of his more memorable fantasies. Definitely. Parija was pointing out landmarks. Here was the great forest, there the mountains, and beyond them, the sea, fields of flowers, roads and villages. This time though, he could feel the rush of air, sweetly scented, rushing past.

"This is a bit like the trip Ananda took us on, over Mummu," he remarked. "It didn't feel quite like this, though. What's that gorgeous smell?"

"Who? Oh, flowers. It's probably the parijata knocking you out."

"You're named after a flower?"

She didn't answer, just coyly peered over the side. It had been a short trip. Their bird was descending, the forest resolving into individual trees, a clearing round a brook. He felt good, naturally happy, told her so.

"You've probably been here before," she informed him mysteriously. "Many lives, many planets. It's that hell you come from that's the problem."

"Earth? It's a great place. What about the Lake Dis..."

"All those infernal machines," she said. "Cars, electricity, filth. People wasting their lives in factories and slaughterhouses. Lies, poverty, hunger, cruelty. The whole place is a reservoir of inauspicious qualities."

"But..."

Their discussion was curtailed as they stepped out of the swan, onto a small field. Following Parija's example, Rob sat down, reclined in the grass by the water's edge. The swan bent its neck and nodded at them gracefully, like everything else it did, then took off again.

"Did you tip it?" asked Robert.

Parija looked skywards at its diminishing form. "They like giving rides. Get bored looking at themselves all day long."

He watched it disappear behind the trees then tried another tack. " 'course it's all very well if you've got flying swan taxis. We haven't, on Earth. That's why we need planes and space rockets and stuff."

She laughed. "There's simply no other way to travel. The only place you'll find flying machines are the hellish underworlds, but they'll never get here with them."

"I did."

"By rocket?"

"Well..."

"It's impossible to get anywhere off Earth in your present age. Just not on. Not allowed. God knows how the Illuminati do it. Maybe it's a boon from Indra or something. Like how we got the bouncy glow-globes – not that we use blackmail. They do all sorts of things they're not supposed to, like drinking the soma-rasa juice. I mean, only devas are allowed to do that, but... they do it anyway." She shrugged, and finished with her hands in the air, as if to say 'what can you do?' "They're a law unto themselves."

"Soma-rasa? Is that the coloured drink where we were dancing?" asked Robert. She nodded. He trailed a hand in the water. "And you're a deva, a kind of goddess?"

"Who else might I be? Tinkerbell the fairy?" His first impressions while dancing had been, as they invariably were, correct.

"Sorry. Everything's so strange and wonderful. It's like you say, I'm just getting my bearings."

"Well, it's very good for you if you get away with drinking it. You get a tingly head, too?"

Rob nodded, the corners of his mouth rising. "I thought you said Earth was a middle planet, not a hellish underworld."

She put a hand on his arm. "Look, I sympathise, really, I do, even if it is what you deserve."

This sounded highly incongruous. He liked the way her hand was placed though.

"It's just a thing you're going through at the moment, happens to lots of planets."

"What is?"

"Kali-yuga. Age of quarrel and confusion."

"Uh-huh"

"Like the seasons. This one's winter."

"Ah"

She took her hand away.

> " *'prayenalpayusah sabhya*
> *kalav asmin yuge janah*
> *mandah sumanda-matayo*
> *manda-bhagya hy upadrutah*

" 'Oh learned one, in this iron age of Kali, men have but short lives. They are quarrelsome, lazy, misguided, unlucky and, above all, always disturbed.'

"*Srimad-Bhagavatam*, current Earth edition, first canto."

"What? It's not that bad, you know. We are quite advanced in many other ways." He paused for thought. "Are things better in other ages then?"

"Yeah. Basically it's a bit more like this. Clean, simple living, bountiful prosperity, people being nice to each other, pious, smart, healthy and long-living."

"How old are you?"

"And polite. What about you?"

"Thirty two. I was, anyway."

"You still are, in your more gross body."

"My what?"

"Never mind. I mean what are you doing here?"

"I don't..."

"I mean with the Illuminati in the first place. To be honest, you seem somewhat inept. Not really in their league."

He sighed. What could he do? Reluctantly he explained the relevant details of steathcomms, Jane, Lakshmi Trading and Ingolstadt, finishing with his 'illumination'.

"Hmm. A fine mess. Do you know where your sister is? No? I thought not. You're completely at their mercy, aren't you?"

"I suppose so."

She tutted. "Best thing's to get something to eat, and sleep on it. That's an Earth expression if I'm not mistaken."

"What is?"

"Sleep on it"

"It is. How do you come to know all about us, but we know nothing of you?"

"Levels of vibration of matter." She gesticulated prettily. "We're on a much higher frequency. Earth's slower and more gross. To you, we're etherial. It's just like your relationship with the hellish worlds. In Kali-yuga, lots of earthlings are on that sort of wavelength. Look at your horror films.

"I try not to, actually."

"There you go, you're on a higher level."

"Ye – oh – ah," he yawned, stretching. The Earth had risen while they had been talking. Now they were sitting in its cool blue light.

Parija arose and went to the edge of the clearing. She reached and plucked a few yellowy-orange fruits from the nearest tree, chucked them at him.

One he caught, the others landed nearby. For a few minutes there was nothing but the sound of squelching, chewing, and sighs of satisfaction. They washed in the brook, then Parija led him by the hand into the forest. Twigs crackled underfoot; a little further off, birds and other animals were scraping and making twittering noises. The light became even dimmer. They arrived at a simple wood and stone cottage.

*   *   *

Oh, what rapture, what bliss! This was *it!* He still felt shudders of that head-to-toe tingle, holding Parija, more intense every time he thought of her, looked at her, said her name; touched her. Parija, Parija! He would travel to the ends of heaven for champaka flowers to decorate her navel. They would be lovers for ever, their minds merging again and again, endlessly in perfect ecstatic union. Her ears he would fill with love-words, her hair, the stroke of his hand a hundred thousand times, her eyes... were looking at him across the table. She seemed calm, confident, detached. Somewhere else.

"Are you going to drink that nectar or shall I have them both?" she asked, waking him from his trance. He gulped. They were seated for breakfast. Sun streamed in through an open window, throwing leaf silhouettes on the surfaces it touched. The shapes moved gently with the wind. He jumped at her command and raised the glass to his lips, never once moving his attention away from her sublime form.

"Look, I have to get into the city soon, meet a friend," she explained. His face fell. "Why don't you hang around here for a while? Get more acclimatised?"

"Yes! Erm, No!, I mean, do you have to go?"

"Mmm." She looked at the sun length on the table between them. "Yes. In about half an hour. It's OK. I'll be back later."

"Later?!?" he cried, unable to completely express his grief. "Where will you be? Can I come?"

For a second, a look of utter distaste crossed her face. She gave Robert the sort of glance generally bestowed on over-affectionate puppies. Then her usual sweet smile returned. "At court. With Kalamba. I'm his mistress," she explained as his face hit the floor, "a society girl." She winked lasciviously.

Robert was destroyed. Everything had gone from polyspectral to black in an instant. An instant. Half an hour. Tomorrow. Years. What was it about time that was bothering him. His brow wrinkled in concentration.

"What is it?" Parija raised her eyebrows.

"An hour, a day, a year here. Being relative. Relative to what?"

"Ah." She fanned her taper-like fingers and counted on them, whispering sibilantly. "Yeah, a day here is the equivalent of... six earth months."

Things went from black to a sort of indescribable void. Robert gulped and half-closed his eyes. "I've been here for a ...*three months*?" She confirmed it with a nod. "Ohh."

"Don't worry," she advised. "Something will turn up. They're bound to get in touch soon enough and tell you why you're here." Parija arose, came round and put her arms round his neck, bending to kiss him.

Stepping outside, she blew another.

Robert smiled and waved faintly. He did not feel able to follow or say goodbye. He was fighting a legion of disturbing and almost completely unfamiliar emotions within.

10   HEAVENLY CONSPIRACY

Trees' shadow
    dynamic and dimmed
        contrasted and clouded
            like a magic carpet
                It's under my feet
            like a magic carpet
        contrasted and clouded
    dynamic and dimmed
Trees' shadow

Robert put the pen down and sighed. He felt torn apart. Writing the poem had been a help, a distraction. It was something he had not tried since his youth.

Useless, though, except as a way to try and forget Parija. Now he had nothing to do, his thoughts were restarting the long spiral downwards into hopelessness. The same stream of questions ran through his mind again. What was happening to Jane? Where was she? How could they escape the Illuminati? What then if they did? Parija in the arms of another man. Parija gone. Parija not his. Head in hands, still seated at the table, Robert began to cry.

A half-hour – or day – later, he rose mechanically, and staggered over to the washing font, splashing water on his baby-face, felt slightly better. He looked around the cottage's room and spotted a bookcase. Turning his head, he read the spines: *Vibhavari Good Food Guide, The Chandralokan Landscape, Heavenly Songs, More Pleasure from Your Body, Conspiracy Facts,* and *Brahma Samhita.* Hmm.

He flicked through *Brahma Samhita*, glancing over a random page.

> 'I worship *Govinda*, the primeval Lord, who is adept in playing on His flute, with blooming eyes like lotus petals, with head bedecked with peacock's feathers, with the figure of beauty tinged with the hue of blue clouds, and His unique loveliness charming millions of Cupids.'

Hmm. Far out. Robert replaced the book, and picked out the tall magenta volume '*Conspiracy Facts*'. Yes, this was what he needed. He took it outside with him to the veranda and found a sitting place in the shade. Coming out here lifted his spirits slightly. It was hard to feel so low amongst the birds and beasts of the forest, chirping, singing and squawking. Harder, but not impossible.

He opened the book again and looked closely at the contents pages. It covered a vast period so far as he could guess from the unfamiliar dates, and a great range of lands and planets, only some familiar. Earth: the major conspiracy here mentioned was The Illuminati. Excitedly, he turned to the relevant section.

The script consisted of unusual lines, bends and squiggles, but somehow he found he was able to read it. At the beginning of the chapter was a warning:

While the publishers have, at great personal risk, made every effort to ensure the information contained herein is completely accurate, it must be understood that the Illuminati, as will be described at greater length later, go to great lengths themselves to present an utterly muddled and confusing account of their structure, aims, and means of operation to all attempted investigations, infiltrations and initiates below top level command

He considered the statement carefully. If it was true, and the Illuminati were really as devious as they appeared, or were made out to be, then what value did any apparent information about them have? The only true knowledge could be in the possession of a 'top level commander', yet, if one were to meet such a person, if Jane and he had actually met the innermost cabal, then what value could be placed on their words? He read on.

Introduction

The conspiritus illuminatus has been existent on Earth for at least some four thousand

189

*years. Its origins are shrouded in mystery
and legend. Several of the most probable and
popular accounts are presented here. As far
as conspiracies go, it rates highly in terms
of longevity, public relations, ruthlessness,
power and wealth, even within the confines
(so far) of a small, backward and insignificant
planet. By its own criteria, it is successful. Its
methods of working are not unusual for such
organisations, typically involving blackmail,
prostitution, murder, kidnap, extortion and
fraud. The ways these methods are applied is,
however, subtle, unusual, and often surreal.
The Illuminati actually worship confusion in the
form of Eris. One in contact with it usually has
no idea of the danger until progression of the
relationship to a point of no return. Illuminati
agents take on all professions as cover.*

*The conspiracy's success
can largely be attributed to:*

*i) its chameleon-like ability to change
form, name and structure incessantly,*

*ii) propaganda purporting itself to be
a ridiculous and unreal make-believe,*

*iii) the loyalty of its operatives. Individuals
working for the Illuminati have in the past
believed themselves to be working for famine
relief agencies, nationalist and state terrorists
or security forces, art galleries, banks, property*

developers, ballet companies, other secret
conspiracies, and Antarctic weather stations.

Robert screwed up his face and rubbed his hands up and down. He was trying to work out whether the book actually contained any actual information, or if he might as well make up his own *Facts*. If he took these statements literally, and to the limit, then perhaps *no-one* could have any idea what was going on. What if its members were so devious that a group thinking itself top level command were actually controlled without their knowledge by another group, in a circular, or recursive fashion? Maybe the whole purpose of his being on the moon was just for him to be lost somewhere. Or confused. Or not on the moon at all. Or all three, or a combination thereof. How could he be sure *where* he was? Or whom to trust? Looking about, seeing no-one but the animals and plants, Robert returned to the book and flicked through a few pages to *history*:

During the early centuries of Christianity,
the Illuminati flourished as the 'men in grey
suits' behind Caesar and the Roman Empire. It
is also stated by some sources that the above's
decline and fall was actually brought about
by an Illuminati desire to re-organise their
management structure. Whatever, the conspiracy
infiltrated various gnostic creeds of the period.
These societies met secretly, and had hidden
signs by which they recognised each other.
Their members were hungry for direct mystical
experience and were therefore ripe pickings for
Augustus Danke (223-285), a revered Illuminati
master. It was his successor, Ramint, who,

through Emperor Justinian's wife, inaugurated
the Empire's absorption of a bowdlerised form of
Christianity, obscuring many of Christ's original
teachings such as karma and reincarnation.

Heavy stuff. Robert put the book down, got up and stretched. This wasn't really getting him anywhere. He might as well go for a walk. Following last night's path, he headed for the clearing, enraptured, appreciating its natural beauty in the fragrant flowers and plants. A russet squirrel crossed his path and stopped to wrinkle its nose before vanishing up the nearest tree. It was just like Earth in many ways, as if all the best parts had been boiled up and distilled; concentrated, like a million midsummer mornings.

The undergrowth thinned. Trees spaced out into long, lazy shadows. He was in the meadow. A few birds and insects flitted about in the misty-dew sprung air. It was perfect. He ran to the brook, picked up a flattish stone, and skimmed it downstream. Bounce, bounce, bounce... eleven, twelve, thirteen... twenty five, twenty six... He gave up counting, turned his head and laughed.

Ah, this was the life. If only Parija were here too. A swim would get him into good shape for the day. He pulled off the elegant cloth wrap he was wearing, hardly pausing to consider how he would tie it up again properly without Parija's assistance, and jumped in. Wow! The cool water lapped at his body, tinkling and splashing round rocks and sand banks. He struck out for the other side, not far, forest coming right to the bank. Even the water felt less dense, his strokes, effortless. He lay on his back, taking water into his mouth, then spurting it up, like a whale fountain. Maybe he could explore a few miles up or down stream. There were lakes, caverns and waterfalls further on. He had seen them from the swan.

On the other hand, just lying here amongst the lilies and lotus flowers could be the most pleasant option. Just drifting. And so, he simply floated, let mind and body drift where they would. The current was slow, and he was content to merely register sense objects between a hot-cool sandwich of sun-haze and water. Trickle, trickle, glug. Chirp-chirp, tweet, caw.

*　　　　*　　　　*

"Ah! There you are, Robert."

"Ugh? Wha?" he replied, somewhere from within his daydream.

"How's your stay so far?" asked Magee. Robert tottered, turned and stood on the riverbed, waist-high in water. A few birds and dragonflies fluttered over the swaying reeds. They were, he guessed, a few miles downstream from Parija's cottage, the clearing in the forest, and his clothes. Magee's upper torso stuck out of the ground, level with Robert's, his lower half, buried into the river bank. He was wearing a large and complicated-looking wristwatch. Magee cleared his throat. "If I seem a little disjointed don't worry. I'm on some damn television thing doing all sorts of time compression stuff."

Robert nodded. "I found out about the relative times. Now, where's Jane, and what am I doing here?"

"Having a bloody good time, presumably." Robert thoughtfumbled through what Magee was trying to say. "Well, if you want to waste a whole one of your earth-days speaking riddles, who am I to stop you? Where's Jane?"

"Doing what she always wanted. Learning a very special type of yoga. Under Ananda. Here. Ingolstadt."

"Ah. And why am I here?"

"Well, it's all part of your initiation, Rob. Get to know how pleasurable life can be with us. A reward, an incentive to do well, if you like."

"Is that it?"

"Ah. Mmm. Now that you mention it, er, there is something you could help us with while you're there. Let me explain."

Robert sighed and put an arm out to lean on a rock.

"It's our scientific division, Rob. We'd like you to help out with that, as it's your speciality. I'll show you round when you get back. Think for a moment. What could Einstein have done with another fifty years? Marconi? Tesla? Bohr? I'm talking life extension. Look at what you've achieved so far. You don't need to die at seventy or eighty. How would you like to live to be two hundred, without disease or frailty?"

"Well, it's a rhetorical question isn't it? Yes. Actually I reckon I could manage to better that quite easily here."

"Your more gross body's still ageing away here at Ingolstadt," said Magee. You wouldn't last two months here. Not to mention Jane. We can't all flit off to the Moon quite so easily, you know. Yet. Your trip's an investment."

"So what do you want?"

"A material we can make good use of. Xthanyte crystal. Look: It's of negligible use to the Chandralokans. To them it's just jewellery. We can really go places with it." He began to gesture persuasively. "You have to take it from the king, Amritamaya. Find out where he keeps it."

Robert started to speak, but Magee was already waving him silent.

"I know what you're thinking. 'Nick the crown jewels? *Impossible*.' We wouldn't send you on a wild goose chase, old boy. All you need are the right tools for the job. Just try this. You're uncomfortable in the altogether aren't you? Want your clothes? Just close your eyes and think of where you left them. Yes? See it in your mind's eye. Now a pyramid over the spot. Hear the sound. See the colours flowing down it."

Robert closed his eyes and tried to remember the river bank. He saw the reeds, the sun's gentle caress on waving grass. A patch of daffodils, his pile of clothes. Above them, he put the pyramid – it seemed to come very easily, very clearly – made it glow red. Let the rainbow humming wash down it. Saw it shine. Saw the whole scene glow, lighter and lighter. Flash!

He was out of the water; grass under his feet. He opened his eyes. He was there, and had to admit, the Illuminati were one up on him, doing it with the mind like this. Quickly he donned the clothes as best he could, then sat on the grass, opposite Magee.

"With complements," spoke the old man. "I said a favourable trade for both parties, didn't I?"

Robert nodded. There was a slight ache in his temple.

"You'll need to practise for a while I'd say. Try small jumps at first 'till you get the hang of it. Don't try any inter-planetary stuff just yet. You won't get back so easily."

Robert felt a hint of menace in what Magee had said, and a worry. Why was he going after crystals? Did they know about the opto-computer too? This could take ages. More time than he had. A sudden chill bit him. He rubbed his hands up and down his upper arms. "What's this Xthanyte crystal like?"

Magee pursed his lips and stared up, into the distance. He put an open left hand out. "He's got one," he gently nodded.

"It just fits, in the palm of your hand." His eyes were slowly closing, his hand bobbing up and down slightly, as if to gauge the weight of it. "You might not be able to actually see it so easily without sunglasses" he warned. "It's effulgent. Gives off a bright, bright light."

"It's not radioactive is it?" asked Robert, still smarting about his television camera.

"No, no, nothing like that. A different, much more complex and benign form of energy. Completely harmless. In fact, it has a healing power."

Robert half-closed one eye and gave Magee a long hard stare. This was complete twaddle.

"It's probably in the palace. Now, you've a very good way of getting in and out. All you have to do is find some pictures, or a description of where it's kept, or a place nearby. You might even approach it on foot. Whatever." He shrugged. "It's up to you."

"What about Jane? I want to see her."

"I'm sure you do." replied Magee, pausing as if relishing his power over Robert. "That can be arranged. Just a moment." He nodded formally and disappeared.

Robert seethed at the thought of being tracked by such an odious presence; touched his forehead. The pyramid had a different feel from the rest of his skin. Cooler. Harder. Not a tattoo at all. Maybe that was how they had picked up on him in the water. An implant. Oh well, nothing he could do about that now. He got up and began to pace.

Then, where Magee had been, there was a shimmering like a heat haze. It settled to a sort of blue mist. In front of him stood Jane.

"Jane!" he called in relief. She looked well, if a little startled. At first, she could hardly believe it was him. He looked so... different. So much younger.

He asked how she was.

She grinned mischievously and stepped towards him. He put his hand through hers.

"I'm always worried about you, you know," he said.

"I know. Me you, too," she replied, telling him how good he looked; he knew that; then pushing her hand through his head, which was eerie. She disapproved of his implant. She was having a good time at Ingolstadt; being a model hostage. They both were. Ananda came forward and put an arm round her. He did not like the possessive way she did it. Jane asked him about what he was doing. He couldn't say much. She knew he was on the moon, anyway. They said goodbye. Robert started trying to give her some advice, telling her to keep her wits about her, but she was fading, gone.

Alistair re-appeared briefly to say goodbye. "And let us know when you've got the crystal. Press the eye-pyramid in your forehead. Don't try to bring it back yourself. Good luck." Then he was gone too; the connection was broken.

Robert sighed resignedly. After another go at dressing properly, he sat down again on the river bank and started to recall Parija's pillow talk of Vibhari city.

11   NEW YOGA

Mist caressed the mountain. In places it was gentle, floating down gullies, over plains, billowing layers, rolling. At times, it blew the falling snow viciously against rocks and crags of the mountain in mini-storms. Through the monochrome beauty not a leaf stirred, nor did small wet nose poke out from icy den. Mid-day sunlight, endlessly diffused through countless layers of cloud, lit the scene dimly. If an observer had sought to describe this place succinctly, they might have settled on 'very' followed by 'high' or 'cold'.

One sheer face of the mountain was broken by glass. There was nothing further out of the ordinary than the Himalayan beauty itself about its shape. The surface though changed abruptly from rock to glass, not ice, perfectly matched, unframed; a window. Although seeming small against the mountain's massive scale, it was a good four metres long by two high. Transparency was hindered by the rock-like contours of its surface, and a tendency to reflect rather than transmit light. But no-one looked in. The observer, hypothetical, might have added 'odd'.

There was no crack in the window; no break, or badly fitted edge. Yet, inside, a cave, where a soft breeze rippled through light cream hessian, blowing folds this way and that, like some vast oversized dress, or incongruously sited desert tent. Thus, the ceiling came intimately low. Down from it swung mobiles – glass butterflies, omms, ankhs and silver shapes, like great monster earrings. Yes – the space was clothed rather than decorated or furnished. Or it grew – branches, leaves...

A curtain blew aside. Behind it, low down, lay a girl. Asleep under white cloth. Hair thrown askew on the pillow. Abruptly she turned, gripping the bedclothes around her. She mumbled, like she was dreaming.

Through a curtain down the other end of the room a woman appeared, apparently no older than the mattress's occupant, but obviously having left girlhood far, far behind, if indeed, it was a quality she had ever flirted with. She turned and left, allowing the sleeper a little longer lie in. Some time later she returned and called.

"Jane, Jane! It's time to get up." Jane shook her head and put a hand to it. Blearily she focused on Ananda. "See you upstairs, yah?", who half turned, then remembered "Oh. Would you like shower, or I could run you a bath?"

Jane's mind struggled with the dilemma. "Err," in a reflex from the classes, she took a deep breath, flooding at least her brain with the oxygen-rich up-ported air; "A bath, please". She relaxed as Ananda smiled slightly, mouthing a kiss as she went. A bath would be nice, and warm, and bubbly. It would effectively put off getting up both in its running and in itself. She sighed, poking a few toes out experimentally onto the ubiquitous oatmeal shag carpet. Ingolstadt was centrally heated. The dining room's open fire was a bonus.

Something kept coming back. Jane knew she had been somewhere it was all at. More 'at' than this. All of it. The place where time stopped, where nothing else mattered, where she hadn't felt she was Jane at all, but a breathless flow into something much bigger. A state without proper description. Somewhere everything had made sense, without needing reason or rhyme. As she tried to remember, a sort of tingly shudder rippled through her body. All that came though, was the image of a melting technicolor eye in pyramid. In one way it was irritating, to have lost that perfectly complete state, where she felt she knew everything, could do anything. On the other hand, if she died today, her life would have been worthwhile. Not that there was any need to. Ananda was promising more of that sort of illumination with the yoga classes.

Yo! She stretched, and struggled out of bed towards the en-suite. Her bathroom was a smaller cave, further into the mountain. She disrobed and stepped into the chuckling pool, lying down again in the womb-like security of the water, closing her eyes.

'Ahh...' She blinked. Cuthbert Jennings stood straight ahead, openly gazing on her.

"Bath all right?" he enquired innocently, leaning to shut off the taps.

"PISS OFF!" she replied. Nonchalantly he complied. That creep was getting right up her nose. Maybe Ananda had some spare martial arts techniques she could employ.

In mixed sorts she finished her bath, dried, dressed and went up. It was Porridge and vol-au-vents again. With royal jelly tea. During breakfast she ignored the men. Meanwhile Caroline and Ananda discussed latest fashions – how to persuade the proles to change their wardrobe more frequently, stock prices and trends, the weather – cloud priming methods, hurricane generation and large-scale insurance swindles. In fact Ingolstadt seemed to be all large-scale except for the standard of conversation. It was like business-talk, or even worse, straight politics. Alistair began an argument about where they should locate the next 'renaissance city'. Caroline got laughed off for suggesting a re-vitalisation of New York, he gave a detailed resumé of his world travels, and Ananda brushed the question aside, saying "Let civilisation go West at its own pace, as it always has done."

"Ha!" exclaimed Caroline. "You suggest we change an interventionist habit of millennia."

Jane drifted again, out of the window and away. It was marginally brighter now, but the mist still rolled, the hail blew.

After breakfast, she began the morning yoga session with Ananda and a handful of pills. "To accelerate progress". Jane had nodded, glad at least to be spared the 'mind-machine' for the moment. The pair of them stretched and rolled in matching black leotards on rubber mats.

Ananda's studio was set at the very top of Ingolsdadt's warren of caves and passages. It was supposed to be an original feature of the mountain, but had been finished off in a smooth modern style. Jutting out into space, half the wall and ceiling were glass.

The flurry of snow continued. Three breathless, aching, quarters of an hour later, Jane sat still, heart thumping, ears listening to another guided meditation into her deep subconscious. 'Peeling away layers, like an onion, feeling your true, all-powerful self in all its naked wonder, rising up through the fifth astral plane, feeling the crackle of energy through your fingertips.' It was quite good actually.

After that they had some concentrated navel- or tip of nose -gazing which she found rather more difficult. It seemed to go on for ever, and she kept getting distracted by all manner of worrisome and irrelevant thoughts. Ananda said that was normal and gave her more pills.

Whatever you called it, she'd had worse jobs. Recently. This was the third month. Ananda said that she'd soon be able to do basic levitation, and that Rob was on a secret mission somewhere and she could speak to him next week. She couldn't quite remember when that had been said. It was hard not to worry. The pills helped sometimes.

In the afternoons, when she was not off on another expedition, Caroline would teach her how to be an Enlightened One, amongst other things, between tokes on a vast Persian hookah. They sat around an ever brewing teapot in her penthouse cave. Jane felt more at ease with Caroline than Ananda, and gradually pieced together a more complete picture of 'The Eye'.

"After Atlantis and Egypt, the Illuminati's next major tool became the Holy Roman Empire" she explained. "This became all the more valuable for the opportunity to control Christian doctrine. When Caesar had done his job, The Eye retreated behind Vatican walls for a few hundred years."

"Wasn't that", cough, "rather restricting?" asked Jane.

Caroline raised her eyes. "Baby, you've really got a lot to learn. Anyhow, The Eye's other wing was off with the Zoroastrians in Persia discovering dualism."

"What's that?"

"It's a perfect description of the world, as far as it goes," replied Caroline. "Good and evil are primary and opposed energies. Evil has just as much chance as good of prevailing."

"But..."

"Look around you girl. This world isn't a holiday camp for most people. They can only take so much reality. The different schools of Dualism held, to varying degrees, that actually Satan must have created the world, or at the very least, he is essentially the ruler of it."

"Hey, that's heavy," said Jane. "No-one rules a free spirit. If you're free in your mind, you're..." she opened her hands and smiled.

Caroline shrugged back. "Anyway, it carried on with the cult of *Mithras* through the Empire's decline; we had a few footholds in early Christian Gnostic creeds too. If someone believes the world's controlled by Satan, that leaves them fairly susceptible to rejecting external authority for something more..." she turned her head, raised eyelids "mysterious."

"Like what?"

"Like... the *Knights Templar*. They were pretty mysterious. Not entirely clear why they were all exterminated in 1307 either. There were some *allegations.*

"What of?"

"Oh, noxious sexual or Islamic practices from the East."

"Like what? Orgies, and Putting contracts out on authors?"

That sort of thing, I suppose."

*   *   *

As weeks passed, the mountain view changed little. Enlightened surely, in many ways, Jane's track on time was all but lost. Her abilities with Ananda in the morning were improving. She became more adept with the 'mind machine'. This device consisted of headphones, a video monitor and a few touch pads. Through it, one could select and direct almost any sort of music, from classical Indian ragas to the most extreme techno-acid noise and heavy metal riffs. It worked partially through the touch-screen, partly through bio-feedback.

Ananda was pleased with her latest sound and put an arm round her briefly, switching the heavy cracking dub through the studio's monitors. "A natural knack you have, my dear girl."

"Yeah, I like it. But what's it for? I mean, it must be worth millions to the music industry."

"Hasn't Caroline filled you in, up to date yet, Jane? Still on medieval cloaks and daggers?"

"She said the Church..."

"Isn't what it used to be I'm afraid"

"So how.."

"Media. In a word, media. Sound. Vision. A few dabbles in the stock market. You'll find most of our energy goes into sounds. Always has done one way or another. People may think themselves as free as they wish, but they still do as they're told. Whatever they listen to. This century it's been radio, TV and record companies"

"For what..."

"So that they buy the right products, do the right things."

"Fight the right wars?" asked Jane

Ananda shrugged and smiled, wickedly, touched a few points on the screen. Immediately, Jane's whole psyche was shaken by a thunderous slamming beat. A hypnotically simple tuneless tune drove its way to her feet. Voices rapped unintelligibly. Then she could make out a word, repeated at the end of every phrase – Eris, Eris, Eris Eris Eris. Something burned in her throat. Her belly felt empty and strained. Ananda was laughing at her. Foul air. She lunged, aiming her head into Ananda's belly. Suddenly an arm gripped round her and threw. The sound stopped. Her shoulder hit the floor and she crumpled. She had been right about Ananda's martial arts abilities. Her mentor looked mean; amused. A torn black headphone lead hung at Jane's side. She panted.

Ananda joined her fingers together in a sky-pointed framework and gave a large nod, or a small bow. "Hail Eris, god of chaos, discord and confusion."

*   *   *

Jane walked with a Pink Panther bendy toy – 'You'll see that he's a groovy cat' – the field was awkward to negotiate but he held her hand steady – 'that he's a gentleman, a scholar, he's an – acrobat' – it was marshy, grabbing their feet, trying to suck them under. 'So now you'll meet the Pink Panther, the Pink Panther' Bombs were going off all around. Red and yellow and blue flashes, throwing bits of mud up into the air – 'Oh he's a panther *ever* so pink' – the air, which was full of smoke, or steam, or mist. 'You'll see that he's a groovy cat'. Her hand hurt. She looked down. The Pink Panther's claws were biting into it. She pulled. He looked up. The ridiculous line-silhouette head was gone. She was looking at a real big cat. An explosion rocked her. This must be the Somme, World War One. "Please, Pink, let go," she said.

The panther jumped into her arms. It was licking her face, the smell of its fishy breath revolting her. "Oh Pink. Pink! Pink!" she shouted. As quickly as he had jumped up, the panther leapt away over the ground leaving Jane confused, uncertain.

Somewhere, a machine gun let off a round of bullets. From high above, a laser beam suddenly shone out, silencing the clatter. Jane looked up. A luminous elliptical shape was slowly descending towards her. It grew steadily larger. She backed away but the object veered, following her as it descended. Her feet were stuck. Desperately, with resignation, she half sat, half fell into a posture of helplessness. Relentlessly, the thing bore down on her. It looked about a hundred feet wide now, glowing like a fluorescent light. Around her, the explosions were still going off. 'Bangloop! Boomsplop!' Gently, it landed. On top of her. All the breath was forced from her lungs. She was pinned to the ground by glowing velvet. Thank God the ground was so soft or she would have been killed. Then, at the moment her pounding heart felt like it was going to give up, the thing opened, and with a suck like a wet kiss, pulled her inside it.

Showers of warm water sprayed Jane from overhead, then blasts of hot air from all sides dried her off. She was in a blue void.

"Jane, Hi! Are you OK?" said a recognisable but disembodied voice.

"Yeah. Just about."

The air before her crackled with shimmering dust as Caroline crystallised into form. "Ugg" she said, dusting herself off.

"Aren't UFO's supposed to take people up on ramps or tractor beams or something?" asked Jane. "I was nearly squashed to death. It seems very clumsy."

"Oh, I wouldn't worry about it," replied Caroline. "Just regard it as a sort of learning experience."

"Learning what?"

"Well, how to cope with difficult situations. Honestly, we had no idea what your subconscious would throw up."

"My subconscious? What about yours? What sort of a twisted mind does it take to drive a hit-and-run flying saucer at people?"

"And cats," added Caroline.

"Cats? You got Pink too?"

"Actually close-encounter buzzing is a great sport. You should try it some time in the distant future."

"The what? I'll be dead."

Caroline smoothed over this minor detail. "One of your re-incarnations of course. That's all they are, you know. Future re-incarnations doing strange things to make the masses evolve. Evolution would never have happened in the first place without time travel.

For a moment, Jane tried to work out where the first place might be, then gave up. There was something nagging her about this sort of logic, but she couldn't fathom what.

"Also," continued Caroline, "I have some good news. Alistair's arranged a holoconference for you and Robert."

Jane was delighted. She would feel a lot better for seeing Rob well. What the hell was he up to anyway?

In another crackle of shining dust, Ananda appeared, and cracked a wink with Caroline. "Ready, girls?" she asked. They nodded. Jane was by now beginning to approach a state where nothing would surprise her.

In front of them, the blue void shimmered. A whole lot of it shimmered like a heat haze, then... a scene appeared which did.

"Oh, Rob. Is it really you?"

He nodded. "How are you?"

"You look so..." they began, interrupting.

Around him was a meadow, full of birds and bees and butterflies. He was on the bank of a brook; on the other side was a magical-looking wood. They stepped forward and pushed their hands through each others.

"I've worried about you." said Robert.

"Me too, you," said Jane. "You look fantastic." She ogled him. "Apart from that stupid tattoo," and pushed a finger into his forehead. "Sound funny too."

"Hey. What's been happening to you anyway?"

"Yoga lessons. Parties. Skiing." Ananda came forward and put a friendly arm round her. "I'm doing OK. And you're on the Moon, no craters, secret mission."

"That's about the long and short of it."

She asked him how long he would be, but Robert seemed disturbed by the question. Not too much longer anyway.

"We'll have to go now," said Caroline. Good luck."

"Blessings!" said Ananda, blowing him a kiss.

"Bye Rob," said Jane sadly. "Take care." She just heard him say goodbye, then the sound went, although his lips were still moving as he faded out. Ananda put her other arm round her as she started to shiver and shake and sniff. Suddenly, with him there and gone so quickly, Jane realised how lonely she felt without any of her old friends.

ANGELS CHÎC

The Moon
  has very little gravity.
Its face blushes.
It's magical!

Sometimes it looks like a banana.

12   VIBHARI CITY

Vibhari city sounded something like a pleasure dome from Kubla Khan's Xanadu. The problems Robert could envisage were plentiful, but he concentrated on just a few. Getting there, finding a pair of sunglasses (did the devas wear such things? He had not seen any yet), not upsetting the locals and getting back. Oh, and time. Without a watch, he could only guess at that, but it seemed to be late morning. He reckoned his arrival yesterday to have been early evening, but it was difficult to tell.

With the same kind of spirit and enthusiasm with which he had practised piano scales as a child, Robert began to exercise his new powers of mind-travel. Here and there he split; he popped up, like some sped-up comic film. He flitted from one side of the field to another.

As his confidence increased, he jumped farther into the forest, back to Parija's cottage and out again. Hey! This was fun. Taking advantage of the low gravity, he tried a few mid-air hovers, but that was harder work. He found the sensation of beginning to fall disturbed his concentration too much; after a few bumps he remained decidedly planet-bound.

Taking a rest, and a few fruit, he mused further on his mission. In some ways perhaps, things were not so hard. See the way Parija had just turned up, out of the blue. And she gave so much...

Shaking himself out of the day-dream, Robert began to create a city in his head. He remembered some of what Parija had told him, and also a book – *Vibhavari Good food guide.* That must have some pictures. In a flash, he was in the cottage again, picking through the bookcase. He plucked the book out and flicked through its pages. There it was: one of the city's finest restaurants. He studied the scene carefully, then closed his eyes and visualised the rippling pyramid above.

Opening them, he found himself sitting at a table on the restaurant's roof. Small marble pillars supported a thick ruby rail running around the perimeter.

Below, above, all around him was spread the city. If it reminded him of anything, it might have been Italy. Even Venice or Rome though, was a dirty slum compared to Vibhari. Nowhere was there a pillar out of place. Flags and canopies fluttered in a gentle breeze. Swans and peacocks graced gardens by rivers, canals and lakes. Each building had its own distinctive style, yet blended perfectly.

Some, like the restaurant, were a mere two or three stories high. Others towered above the skyline, dripping with trellises, balcony gardens and bridges.

Not more than half a minute later, a waiter appeared, running up a sweeping staircase on the side of the building. He was wearing loose silk pants and shirt of fine cut. The colours in his clothes changed with the angle of view. His shoes were plain pointed black.

Robert was about to decline the proffered menu when he realised how hungry he was. "I'll have whatever you recommend" he told the waiter. "Something full of energy."

Immediately, a drink was placed before him. The waiter nodded and pointed to the menu. "I recommend number twenty three, sir" he said, and went.

Robert took the drink and turned to look over the restaurant. There were only a few diners besides himself, groups of friends and lovers lingering over drinks and deliciously fragrant meals. The sun was not yet high. It must be late morning.

Soon, his food arrived. It comprised a variety of delicious vegetable dishes with different sorts of breads and rices, followed by a plate of cakes and sweets. For payment, the waiter accepted a small golden trinket from Robert's tunic, and told him where he might find a market into the bargain.

"And what about the palace of Amritamaya?"

The waiter gestured past the opposite side of the restaurant. "Over there, through the forest on top of that hill."

Robert thanked him and staggered out. That is, had expected to stagger, but actually drifted much as usual in the low gravity. Bouncing down the steps, he picked his way through narrow busy streets towards the indicated market-place. From verdant shadow, he came out into it suddenly: a sun-filled open space of white stone and marble. Trees sprouting round the oval circumference gave a pleasant shade, and a fountain in the middle, a focus to the place.

The stalls themselves were simple enough, but the merchandise on them a king's ransom. Robert meandered in a daze. Conscious of time passing, he at last picked on one of the stalls and asked its owner if he knew the whereabouts of a pair of sunglasses. The deva guided Robert by the elbow to another merchant, who sold head gear. All manner of hats, wigs, nose- and ear-rings were arranged on a framework of cane and bamboo.

The merchant reached across the display and handed a black circular band to him. On one side, a round knob stuck out.

Robert tried it on; a flexible, stretching, perfect fit. The knob controlled level of opaqueness, a useful feature. He paid with another golden trinket, thanked the seller, and moved on.

Getting out of the circus, he found a quiet spot to disappear from, and visualised the palace hill. Opening his eyes, he found himself there, in a patchy gladed wood. Little by little, Robert looked ahead and jumped. As he rose upwards, the vegetation became more cultivated. Beneath his feet grew soft lawn; around him, flower-beds. Ahead was the palace.

He gulped at its sheer extravagance. It was all gems, looming up like a mountain of prism-like diamond. Looking for the Xthanyte Crystal here could take forever. An idea struck him. Parija! Not that she was ever far from his thoughts. He turned the thought around, examining it from all angles. Well, it was a start. Eyes shut, he made a picture of her as she had left that morning. "Parija" he whispered, seeing her, distantly, under that shimmering pyramid.

He found himself inside a dark place, reached for the visor and turned it down. He could hear voices. A slit of light showed him to be behind a curtain of some kind. Cautiously, he peered through.

Parija was reclining on curious mirrored cushions with a deva, presumably Kalamba. Even amongst demi-gods he looked aristocratic, handsome. She was fully clothed, which for her was not very. They were laughing and chatting. Lovers' talk, thought Robert jealously. Kalamba seemed to be telling a long and amusing story about the incompetence of a certain minister. Parija was interrupting him to poke fun, flirt and pour more drinks. Things which, amongst others, she was very good at. All the time, Robert felt like jumping out and screaming at them. Eventually the story finished. Kalamba explained that he had business to attend to, and picked up his jacket from the floor. They kissed, comprehensively. Parija pouted at him as he left.

Robert was left wondering whether this had been a good idea or not when Parija got up, suddenly very calm and cool. She crossed to the window and looked out scrutinisingly, then returned to the cushions, plumped up and tidied them. She sat down on one cross-legged, facing the window, her left side to Robert.

A very low sound came from her. He could not believe she was actually making it herself. Her face began to ripple horribly, as if it was cloth, blowing in the wind. Robert felt sick. He felt afraid now, as well as angry, wanted to rush out and grab her. Transfixed, he could hardly move a muscle.

Silence. A quiet that seemed to ring out with so much force he wondered just how loud the sound had been. Parija's face was still. No. Parija's face, Parija's *head* was not there. It had been replaced with another's. Older. Darker skinned. He knew it from somewhere... Then she spoke. He knew her all right. It was Caroline Steinbeck.

"Hi P.J. How's things?" came her Jewish New York drawl.

The voice, though not the head, changed back. "Seem to be working out fine, Carol. What about you?"

"Nuts. Same as ever. You seem to get all the plum jobs."

"Ha! Like trying to pull a fast one over dear Robikins?"

"Come off it. You must have him round your little finger by now."

"I have, actually. It was a pushover. He's very sweet, isn't he?"

Caroline laughed. "Not from what his kid sister's been telling me, and the CIA files. Apparently all he cares about is his work. *Machines!*" She grimaced.

"Well, I'm his work now, ha; the loving machine."

Robert felt himself flush. He was right. Parija had been waiting for him at the dancing. This whole thing was a put-up job, a honey-trap.

"Alistair briefed him about the gem a short while ago," said Caroline. "He should be mind-hopping around now, looking for it."

"Doesn't he know where it is?" asked Parija.

"We thought it might be best if he found out by himself. Maybe you could tell him. He's probably not going to take it too well."

"Mmm yah, see what you mean. And I've got no axe to grind, have I?"

"Quite. So, I'll leave it to you."

"No problem. I should be back at the cottage to see him quite soon."

"Great. Bye then."

The figure put her thumbs and forefingers together in a triangle, or representation of a pyramid. Caroline's face melted away, replaced by Parija's; 'a distinct improvement,' thought

215

Robert. 'You two-faced bitch.' Well, whatever the rights and wrongs of the betrayal and duplicity he had just witnessed, there was no going back just yet. Not to Earth anyway. He had no choice but to see it through, even though it was beginning to sound like less and less of a picnic. *Gem* now, not crystal...

Parija got up and left by the door. Robert came out from his hiding place and surveyed the room. His cover had been a tapestry, rather in the style of *Déjurné sur l'herbe*. In fact, the whole room was similarly furnished, as a boudoir, designed, it seemed, for one purpose.

Sickened and numb, he decided to put on a purposeful air and have a quick look around the palace anyway. Opening the door, he stepped out into a wide passageway. No-one saw him leave the room. He turned left, walking briskly. The style here reminded him slightly of some merchant bank in the City – flowing plants, marble, fountain-pools. He had visited a few in the course of his last job. The corridors turned and twisted. He ascended a wide flight of transparent stairs. Before him was a great arched entrance into a cavernous hall of indescribable splendour. A guard stepped forward and blocked his way with a hefty stick.

"What brings you to the court of Amritamaya, ruler of the Moon planet, O noble stranger?"

Robert had his answer ready. "I am just a humble message boy sir. Do you know where I might find the noble Kalamba?"

"Kalamba, eh? Lord of the water and rivers. He's through there, in audience with his majesty. You'll have to wait until he comes out." The guard had relaxed his grip on the weapon. "Please wait here." He indicated a comfortable bay-window seat beside the door. Robert moved over to it, then turned and asked if there was somewhere he could wash himself after his

journey. The guard pointed to a small door. "Through there."
Robert thanked him, went through it and mind-hopped back
to Parija's cottage.

*   *   *

Thankfully, he got back before her. Nothing
had changed except that the sun was higher
in the sky. He sat outside and waited.

Presently, the soft flapping sound of a large bird alerted him
to Parija's arrival. As before, she landed in the clearing, then
walked along the cottage path as the swan took off again. Robert
forced himself to run towards her; they met in an embrace and
a fluster of insincere babble from him.

"How do you call the swan if you suddenly want to go
somewhere?" he asked as they separated.

"Ah-ha," she replied enigmatically, tilting her head back, half
closing her eyes and looking down her nose. Robert laughed.
She shook her hair free. "Why are we heading inside on a day
like this?"

"To get some drinks?" suggested Robert. Parija agreed.

Loaded up with a few bags, they continued along the forest
path towards a place she described as ideal for a picnic. On the
way, she asked if he had been able to discover any more about
the reason for his trip. Robert did not disclose his meeting with
Magee, and said that he remained perplexed. As they walked,
squirrels and rabbits scampered out of their way, up trees, down
warrens and into bushes. Robert realised how relaxing were
the sounds of Chandraloka. Even in the city, there had been
no machines or motor-vehicles, only the sounds of birdsong,
bees, and conversation – sung, not spoken, in a language he

was beginning to appreciate more and more, whatever the circumstances.

He deliberately refrained from asking what she had been up to that morning and, tactfully, she did not tell him; instead, asking how his morning had gone. He told her he had spent it swimming and sunbathing. "I had a look through your bookshelf too," he admitted. "*Conspiracy Facts* was quite interesting."

"Oh, that," she said. "Might have known you would try and find out more about The Eye. It's a very dull book really. Out of date, too. It must be oh... six hundred years behind Earth times."

"How long do you live?" asked Robert. "Everyone looks about sixteen."

"What, at the dance?" said Parija. "Maybe we are. You know, a birthday party." She giggled, then became more serious. "Actually we live about ten thousand years. We're born with one of these." She indicated her flower-garland. "And only get pregnant once, near the end of our life." She poked a finger into Robert's chest. "So you needn't worry. I'm not that old. When the garland fades... your time's up," she finished sadly.

Robert thought for a while. "So how... I mean, what then? Is that it?"

"What you mean is, what happens when we die? Do we re-incarnate here on Chandraloka?"

"Yes. Do you keep coming back as demi-gods, and us as humans?"

"Not necessarily. It all depends on *karma*. Whatever actions I perform in this life determine my next body. 'As the embodied soul continuously passes, in this body from boyhood through youth to old age, the soul similarly passes into another body at death. A sober person is not bewildered by such a change.'

Usually, we fall back down to a human life on Earth."

"What about us?"

"If you die in the mode of ignorance you take a lower birth, like an animal. Die in the mode of passion – that's probably you, Robert – and you get another human body. Leave your body in the mode of goodness and you end up somewhere like this."

"Oh."

"That's exactly what the Illuminati are trying to do, both individually, and as a whole. Either get here themselves through yoga, or establish their pernicious influence on us."

"I can't see myself as much of an agent."

"You're maybe a better one than you think."

"So what does the book leave out?"

"Pretty much everything after the fourteenth century. With the demise of the Knights Templars they formed the OTO."

"What's that?"

"*Ordo Templi Orientis*, a secret society with great influence in American politics. Sometimes accused of black magic and devil worship. Though not by anyone very long-lived afterwards. It's said the late President Kennedy didn't get on too well with them. They do a lot of work with intelligence agencies. Perfect cover for their sort of activities."

"Oh, surely," said Robert. "you're not saying they run everything. I mean, we in the West do live in an open democracy, bad as it is."

"The West?" Parija laughed at his naïveté. "I'm not saying the Illuminati are the only ones," she said. "But I'd sooner believe in fairies than a fair democracy. There are powerful and silent forces who control your society. Both they and the masses they control have long given up any deep philosophical inquiry and are completely absorbed in simply enjoying themselves. The people are thoroughly controlled by the media and educational institutions."

"What? Every reporter and teacher on Earth an Illuminati agent?"

"More or less, yes. If they're co-operating with the system. You don't need to know you're working for The Eye. They're in charge at the top. That's all that matters. Those who might be able to question and object have been bought with large salaries or buried within bureaucracies. Your 'free democracies' are rapidly turning into rigidly controlled dictatorships just like in that Earth book, '1984'."

"Oh," said Robert. He had not really thought about things like that before, and was at a bit of a loss for words.

"Ah, here we are!" said Parija as they suddenly came out of the forest into brilliant sunshine. It was very hot, but not uncomfortable. Chandraloka never was. They looked along a vibrantly colourful valley. He had not noticed that they had been climbing up so far; there had been no effort in it, no sweat. Now they gazed down at the breathtaking view.

She pulled at his hand. "Just a little further, come on."

At last, they settled amongst soft grass and heather and got the picnic out. It was a light spread: just a few nuts, fruits, pastries and other snacks. And plenty of soma-rasa drink. Robert's thirst had never been so acute. Nor so well satiated. He gazed at Parija's perfect form in rapture. Her breasts especially, he could have contemplated all day, were it not for her face... Why did she speak so candidly of The Eye's evil exploits? Did she seek to corrupt him? And for all that, working hand in hand with Caroline Steinbeck – leading light in an organisation she vilified and warned him of. How he wished he could trust her again. As if fate was teaching him a lesson for never having fully confided in anyone, now he had no-one to confide in.

There was no way round it. He had to find out where the Xthanyte crystal was somehow.

"How was your morning?" he asked casually.

She spared him the gory details. Little by little, the conversation turned to the court of king Amritamaya.

As Parija was talking, a butterfly landed on her wrist. They looked at the intricate glistening patterns of its wings. Robert kissed her neck. "Nothing on the Earth or Moon compares with your beauty, my love." She kissed him back.

"Except, perhaps, the king's inner court."

"Inner court. What's there?" he asked. Have you ever seen it?"

"Oh, no. Only his wives and most intimate guests go there. It is said there are whole rooms full of fabulous jewels. The windows, seats, floor – everything fashioned from gems. You can't begin to imagine it..."

"And..." This was crazy. She knew what he wanted to know. He knew she was waiting to tell him. And yet they were pussyfooting around like... like new lovers, dancing closer, one step at a time. It suited her. He nestled his head deeper into her lap. "What's the most beautiful thing there? Is it a crown or something?" He knew already, but her answer startled him.

"The Syamantaka jewel. Brilliant like the Sun. Bestows good health and fortune on all those around it. Originally a gift from the Sun-god, Surya to the Earth-king Satrajit."

"Does it go by any other name?"

"I understand certain parties refer to it as the Xthanyte crystal. It is guarded by four lions at the North and South doors of the topmost room and is set on a diamond pillar at the centre of a deadly snake-pit."

13 YOGEEK

Jane did not get much chance to dwell on her loneliness. The next morning after breakfast, Cuthbert announced that his term as servant was up. She had not realised his position to be temporary. By a majority of four to zero with one abstention, she was elected cook, cleaner, secretary, laundress and general slave of Ingolstadt. In some ways this was not so bad. She felt better occupied, and now had legitimate reason for access to some of the place's more interesting nooks and cubby holes. Even the laundry room had its secrets to disclose. Alistair's trousers came in regularly covered in sand; on one occasion she found a kipper in one of the pockets.

The kitchen was long, light and airy; one of the few rooms with windows that opened, letting in gusts of thin, icy air. They ran down its length, above the marble work-surface, giving a great view of the snow and mist. It seemed they had arrived on an unusually clear day. The glacier was now seldom visible.

Alistair complained a few times about her refusal to cook meat. In the end he grudgingly had to accept her request to prepare it himself, preferably not in her kitchen. She later learned from Cuthbert that Alistair was permanently excused from the cooking rota on account of his tendency to produce nothing but toast, and steak and chips *ad nauseum*.

Of course, there was not too much drudgery. Every kind of labour-saving device was there to save her precious time. Including the sort which took twice as long to clean afterwards than the time it saved. Jane found the floors rather novel. Divided into narrow strips, imperceptible through the heavy shag pile, they turned over automatically in the night and were cleaned by some mechanism underneath. Small objects thus dislodged turned up in a box in the lobby.

One area she had no wish to investigate at all was Cuthbert's suite, set way back, deep into the mountain, presumably without natural light. Neither Ingolstadt's own deep humming, nor the air conditioning unit made any difference. Unnatural sounds, below the threshold of precise identification filtered out at intervals. Like little cries or howls. And high pitched electric motors. But the smell... nauseating though faint, reminded her of occasions when, absent-mindedly, she had thrown a torn-off fingernail into the gas fire. Back home.

"Hi babe!" came a voice behind her. She gasped and whipped round, startled out of her skin. It was him, still wearing the same ridiculous uniform and jeans. From the smell, exactly the same. Jane swallowed. Her skin prickled.

"If you don't mind..." she began.

He interrupted, winking slyly. "I couldn't help sneaking up on you like that. You look so sexy when you're being furtive."

She started to back away, but behind her was the wall. He closed in, holding his body against hers, sliding a hand round her bottom.

"Just piss off! OK!"

"I know you're intrigued what I keep in there," replied Jennings, pulling her right hand down between them.

Swiftly, she brought her knee up hard. He cried out and staggered back. Jane ran, screaming insults behind her. Ran fast, as far as she could.

Ananda's yoga studio was the highest place she could get. Jane pushed her way in, and slammed the door shut. She panted. Could she hear steps? Running? Laughter??? Bewildered, she realised that she herself was laughing. At what, she could not guess. Just collapsed on the cushions.

Blinking a little, she became aware of Ananda, ten feet in front of her. And four off the ground. Legs and arms crossed, eyes closed. This raised a number of questions concerning matter, mind and reality. Jane decided to try and keep things simple.

"Er.. hi Ananda."

"Hi Jane. Everything OK?" While speaking, Ananda opened her eyelids. Beneath them, her eyes were completely white, like pearls.

Jane gulped. Everything was not OK. She was upset and getting upsetter.

"Well, no. Actually I think I could do with a break. Cuthbert just tried to rape me. You're floating in the air with no eyes. Robert's on another planet, and I'm stuck here out of touch with the rest of the world."

Ananda tutted, then sighed. "Men. You're taking too much notice of appearances, my dear. Come sit here. We'll do the fish breathing exercise. You need to lighten up."

"Stuff the fish breathing exercise! What are you going to do about that pervert downstairs? And when are you going to let me out?"

"Let you out? You make it sound like we treat you as a cat. Of course you're free to go out. Robert's out right now, is he not?"

Jane thought she heard a hint of a threat in her brother's name. She might be allowed an outing, but he was the leash that would hold her. "We go out all the time." This was true. Often, her captors were gone hours, or even days at a time. And she had never before explicitly demanded to do the same. "We're quite fond of a particular Island just off Greece. Go there quite a lot." So that was where they got their suntan. "Why don't you come with me and Caroline tomorrow?"

"Yes, I'd like that."

"Poor soul!" said Ananda, uncharacteristically sympathetic. "It's no wonder you are not yourself, cooped up inside with us all the time."

"Something lifted in Jane's being. She felt somehow relieved of a heavy burden. A growing, insidious feeling of claustrophobia blew away with Ananda's words. She had not noticed its descent, but its departure was invigorating.

"As for Cuthbert, I'll see he does not bother you any further. We do indulge him somewhat, with his being so old."

"Old? He doesn't look more than twenty."

"Appearances dear. Don't count for a thing." And with that, Ananda shut her eyes, continuing to float four feet up in the air."

*   *   *

Jane had not yet been out apart from that memorable trip down the glacier. But she had been in some kind of touch with the rest of humanity. That strange section of it anyway involved in the media. The nearest thing Ingolstadt had to a TV lounge was Alistair's office. Large and light, it was arranged in descending concentric contours of chairs and equipment, culminating in a sunken sofa area at the room's nadir. It was here that Alistair spent much of his time, ploughing through a forest of newspapers, cracking pistachios and occasionally feeding live tropical fish from a network of tanks and pools to Felix. Jane had only recently been delighted to discover the cat's presence, and vied jealously for his favours with Alistair. She achieved only variable success however, perhaps because of her more squeamish nature.

Reception of television was possible from around the globe. Several people at once could watch different channels on the paper-thin screens, hearing their own soundtrack on cordless headphones.

Nothing much had changed. At first, Jane came regularly to watch news and documentaries, but then her interest dwindled. There was no mention of her and Rob's disappearance, of course; after a few weeks she would only stick around for the odd film over joints with Caroline.

Her yoga sessions with Ananda continued most mornings. They were less regular now she had so much else to do, but she was still supposed to practise on her own whenever she could.

The Greek outing was a great success. Being yet without any teleport siddhi of her own, Jane linked arms with Ananda and Caroline. They were transported to an idyllic beach in a secluded cove. The sun was a tonic. She swam, lay around, and explored the rocky hills with Caroline all afternoon. Ananda had gone to find Roisín, a 'great friend' of hers. Later on, they all met up for a restaurant meal in the town. Roisín turned out to be a 'top operative,' too, one of the most devastating beauties Jane had ever seen. Clinging to her was a drunken, unremarkable looking man in his forties introduced as Arron.

"Shalom!" said Caroline, greeting him with a kiss on the cheek. "Our man in Mossad," she explained, on his next of many trips to the gents. Dining, drinking and dancing to a live jazz band until late, the day left Jane aglow and refreshed.

*   *   *

Newly inspired, she put her all into Ananda's yoga exercises, keenly looking forward to the day when she too might levitate, and travel at the speed of mind. The neglected housework was not remarked on by anyone much. They were not the most domestic of cave-mates. Ananda increased her drug dosage, and began to initiate her into techniques of tantric practice. Some of this involved concentration on mandalas – intricate designs of geometric shapes. Some involved partaking of food and drink Jane considered rather dubious at best. There was more use of the mind machine. Her state of mind was certainly going places. Some, she had visited before, vowing never to return. On one occasion, the walls and floor disappeared; she was left with a vision extending all around, far into a shimmering distance of insubstantiality. "Your kundalini is rising; your chakras opening," said Ananda. Jane felt something growing within her, as if she were on the verge of becoming a new person. But also, she was afraid. Where was the old Jane she thought she knew and loved? Was she in danger of losing part of herself? Between stretches of clarity, a terrible darkness took over sometimes when she was alone. All sorts of fears – real and imaginary, there was no telling which – stalked behind her. Some, she could grapple with. Others lay half-formed, inarticulated, subconscious.

"And open!" said Ananda.

Jane opened her eyes and blinked. Sitting on the floor, she could not remember what she had just been doing.

"Relax," said Ananda.

Jane fell automatically into the deep-breathing exercise she had learnt months before. Perhaps she had been hypnotised.

"Keep focused," said Ananda. This meant she was supposed to keep concentrating on whatever it was they had just been concentrating on. Or perhaps there was a more literal meaning. Ananda stood between her and the snowstorm through the window. In one graceful movement she peeled off of her leotard. Jane's heart started to beat rapidly. There was a certain look in Ananda's cold blue eyes. Hunger.

"The next exercise we will do without clothes," said Ananda, smiling slightly.

Jane had more than an idea what the next exercise would involve. Something she had felt under the surface for a while. She was certainly no prude, but... Ananda's action catalysed her resentment. She knew she stood no chance in argument and did not try it.

"I'm through!" she announced. "I'm sick of your yoga, sick of your drugs, sick of your mind machine. I'm sick of you! Forget it!" Jane picked herself up and left.

*   *   *

Caroline was nowhere to be found. At last Jane tried Alistair's office. She was there, with him, sat at a long console, up, opposite what had been the window.

They were both surprised at her arrival. Caroline, especially, looked as though she had been caught 'at it' in some way.

"Are you, er... looking for Ananda?" she asked.

Jane took a sharp intake of breath. She leant back and gripped the door frame. Where the window had been was an angled view down onto the floor of a busy stock exchange.

"No, I wasn't." She felt giddy, but realised it was a hologram and gingerly stepped into the room, keeping her eyes on the surfaces nearby.

Alistair touched a key on his console and the scrolling data on the screen before him froze. "I thought you were having a special session today, Jane. Getting off the ground at last."

"What's it to you, anyway? Actually I was looking for Caroline."

Caroline began to answer and half got up, but Alistair placed a hand on her shoulder and interrupted. "I'm sorry, we're both occupied with some rather important business at the moment." He placed the hand back on Felix, stroking rhythmically.

'Below' them, hundreds of figures scurried about in their hive. Their uniform was consistent: white or striped shirt, bright tie, short hair, dark trousers. Their noise and shouts created a fast, passionate atmosphere.

Almost the whole of the room was ablaze with data; names of companies and commodities, prices of each flickering from moment to moment as its value changed.

"What important business? Don't you own everything already?"

Caroline tapped at her keyboard and turned to Alistair. "Cocoa down three and a half cents. Sell."

Alistair tapped a few keys and responded. "Rubber and steel, too. Sell steady 'till they go."

"We don't own everything," said Caroline, still typing away. "just control a few strategic markets."

"Then what are you doing?" asked Jane.

"It's Black Monday," responded Alistair.

"You what?"

"Just a little cyclic crash in the ups and downs of the global capitalist economy."

Jane looked down at the wall data more closely. Half- and quarter- cent at a time, the prices were dropping. "Are you doing this?" she asked.

Caroline, straight-faced, nodded.

"Why?"

"It's just one of those adjustments that have to be made now and again to stay on top."

"But, what about the bankruptcies? What about third-world farmers? If their prices collapse they'll starve."

Caroline and Alistair sighed, looked up and at each other. Alistair turned back to his screen. "Buy all Canadian gold," he instructed. The prices were falling now five and ten cents at a time.

"I'm not getting through to you, am I?" said Jane. Before them, the stock market hologram had changed. There were more jobbers on the floor. The pace was getting frantic. They were holding arms up, making urgent signals to sell.

"Thought you were all for a crash," said Alistair. "With your trendy green-anarchist ideals."

Jane's mouth opened to reply, then shut again. Opened then shut. Like one of the tropical fish that swam around them. How the hell did he know what she thought? Who did they think they were? God? The clamour of shouts was making it hard to think. Alistair and Caroline were ignoring her, engrossed at their consoles. This was a fine place to expect sympathy. Indignantly, Jane stormed out, on the way shouting a suggestion to the pair of them that they attempt a feat generally considered physically impossible.

Now she was really through. All those doubts and anxieties and fears were gone. Everything was quite clear and simple. The whole lot of them could go to hell without her. She would rather die than stay trapped here. There must be some way out. She strode away with fury, ready to strike out at the slightest provocation.

Without having consciously planned it, Jane found herself outside Cuthbert Jenning's door. A momentary twinge of nervousness passed through her. "Go on" she urged herself, and opened it with a twist and a kick.

Revealed was a wide light passageway, surprisingly clean considering its occupant. The floor was tiled. There was a hospital-like smell of disinfectant masking another, more repulsive, odour: the whole area felt like some kind of clinic. Down the corridor on one side was a series of doors. She tried the first: a toilet. The next room was almost completely empty, except for a bed, chest of drawers and wardrobe. It might have been the sanatorium, but Jane could see that the bed had been slept in, and no-one at Ingolstadt was physically ill. Small and bare as the room was, it had to be Cuthbert's. The next held shelves of medical supplies. The one after that seemed to be a laboratory. As she entered, the door closed itself behind her. It was very cold, maybe just above freezing. Jane folded her arms over her chest. All she had on was a leotard, leggings and trainers. Not enough. Along the benches were fluid-filled beakers, bottles and tubes, various electronic instruments. She touched one and jumped as a motor whined. It was stirring the murky contents of a glass bowl. Behind her came a couple of squeaks. White rats. She felt the perspex cage. At least it was heated. Further along was a window. It looked into another room. A prison, lengthy, running alongside the lab. In it she could see cages. Within them, animals – rabbits, sheep, cats and dogs. Some monkeys. And two young men inside a couple of foreign-looking phone boxes. White, twentyish, in jeans and T-shirts, slumped, eyes closed. Jane hammered at the glass with her fist. No response. It was probably mirrored. Maybe double-glazed. Perhaps if she could get them out they would help her. She ran to the end of the lab. Another door. She opened it and stepped through. This room was circular, smaller, and just as cold. Around its edge were seven couches, or beds, built in to the room. Over the head of each was a video monitor. Further down, a transparent cover. She looked at the first. It bore a label: 'C. Jennings/CNS'. Underneath was an old, wrinkled man. Wires and tubes ran all over the body, which was clothed only in a pair of blue shorts. The top of his head was hairless, and completely covered in electrodes.

She backed away and cast a glance over the other beds. Only one more was occupied. She approached it.

'R. Ashley' read the label, and underneath was Robert, in a similar condition. Jane screamed, the primeval, deafening sound of a mind turned wild. She got hold of the cover and pulled, hard. It would not budge. She looked for an implement to hit it with. The room was bare. Still screaming, she ran back into the lab, saw a retort stand clamping some equipment together. Grabbed it, complete with clamp, and started swinging it round by the rubber tube. Smash! went a bench of equipment. She took hold of the metal rod, and swung the heavy base into the window, breaking it loudly. Her frenzied screaming never stopped as she ran back into the round room. Hard as she tried, though, Robert's cover resisted her blows. Suddenly she was grabbed from behind and the retort stand prised from her fingers. Someone pressed the back of her neck. In agony, she fell to the ground, shocked. The screaming stopped. Above her stood Caroline, Alistair and young Cuthbert. Alistair and Caroline knelt down on her, pinning her limbs immobile. Cuthbert stood, squirting a hypodermic syringe into the air at eye level, grinning. She struggled, but nothing was moving.

"Let me go, you bastards!" she shouted.

Alistair tutted, and shook his head. Cuthbert bent down, syringe poised. Jane screamed again, very loudly.

Then everything went black.

14 THE JEWEL THEFT AT AMRITAMAYA'S PALACE

"I think our esteemed Robert lacks courage," said Rohini, queen of Chandraloka. "It is already half past six. Parija, you must have scared him off – or enticed him with the promise of another night in your arms."

Parija looked up to protest, but king Amritamaya was already defending her. "Don't worry, darling. He will come. The court geomancer has confirmed it. Parija has done all she needed to."

The king and his wife were as full of youth and beauty as any deva, but more finely and formally attired. He had dark hair and a moustache; she, blonde locks which she frequently rubbed over her many dazzling rings and chains of jewelled gold. The three of them had been sitting in the courtroom since late afternoon. Parija put her head back into reach of a small mango-juice waterfall and took a drink. She was bored and nervous. In front of them was a large square picture frame. Inside, it showed the Syamantaka jewel, shining brilliantly on its diamond pedestal, dripping with liquid gold. For the past two hours, nothing except the snakes had moved. They slid and hissed and occasionally waved their tongues.

Rohini spoke again. "So we shall still fly to the lakes of milk, honey and sugarcane juice tomorrow?"

"We shall fly in celebration!" said the king. "The Bavarian Illuminati will no longer pose any threat to the demigods. Lulled into complacency by the immediate success of their theft, they will never suspect our infiltration. Their plans to expand activities off-Earth are doomed."

Far away, a gong sounded. One of the hall's mighty doors opened and a guard announced the entrance of the Prime Minister. His steps on the marble floor echoed around the huge space as he approached the king's presence. He bowed.

"Greetings, oh blessed sovereign, source of life for all. Hail, oh all-pervading deity of the mind, source of potency for herbs and plants!"

"Good to see you, Paramasthi," said the king. "You have not missed much." He indicated a comfortable seat at his side, which the minister took. "Have there been any further readings on the gem's recovery?"

The minister nodded. "A casting of sand from the base of Mount Meru was made today. It indicates that conditions on Earth at the moment are far too degraded for the jewel to remain there. There is a strong indication of recovery, but by what means... is not known."

The king thought for a moment. "Perhaps their mystic power will be insufficient to transport it. The pawn, Robert, is particularly weak in that regard. It will take all his strength to merely move the gem a small distance." His subjects made murmurs of agreement.

"Look!" shouted Parija. "There he is!" Six feet above the snake pit, on a level with the jewel, Robert was briefly flashing into sight, and out again. He was wearing the sun shades, looking terrified. They watched, spellbound, as he solidified, hovering precariously. A lion roared and padded into the room. It stared up at him, snatching with outstretched claws. Another joined it from the opposite doorway. Robert raised his feet, floating almost upside down to avoid them, grimacing with effort. Below, the snakes raised themselves; they hissed and spat venom. Back and forth around the room's perimeter the lions paced. One ventured a foot over the snake pit, then withdrew. They were making a noise that sounded like death for the hunted.

Robert stretched out his hands and touched the Syamantaka jewel. As he did so, his whole being changed. He became effulgent himself, shining from every inch of skin, luminous through his cloth. He arose; the jewel moved up with him. At the movement, bells started ringing; heavy metal shutters shot down over the windows and doorways. Still, the jewel lit everything with an almost painful brightness, dollops of liquid gold splashing down on the pedestal. His mouth turned into a smile. It opened slightly. As Robert turned in the air, one leg got too close to a lion. With a ferocious roar, it stretched out a paw and clawed his calf. A chunk of skin tore away, bleeding. The lion licked its claw hungrily; its mate ran round to the other side of the snake -pit. Robert was in agony, screaming and yelping with pain. He turned, right way up, and knotted his brow in concentration.

With a shimmer like heat-haze, he, and the jewel were gone.
The room plunged into darkness.

*   *   *

Robert had woken up alone, on the hill above the beautiful
valley. Disturbed a little, but not too surprised by Parija's
disappearance, he had thought out his plan of action, and
started practising mid-air hovers. After attaining reasonable
proficiency, he had gone straight to the inner court as
described, and now found himself back on the hillside.

The sun was low in the sky. Almost as low as when he
had arrived yesterday. He had been here nearly a day. Nearly
six Earth months. His head and leg hurt, but the pain was
lessening by the minute. Amazed, he watched as the torn
tissue grew back over itself. In a short time it was completely
healed. He tried walking on it; it was fine. Lovingly, he gazed
at the crystal, surrounded by a growing pool of gold. His dull
headache was gone too. If this was what the jewel could do to
a wounded leg... what could it not do? He held it to his chest,
feeling its power, gathering strength. He had to go, very soon.

He would have preferred somewhere else, but with Jane stuck
there, it would have to be Ingolstadt. All he could hope for was
surprise. Taking one last, long, lingering look at Chandraloka,
he shut his eyes and visualised one of Ingolstadt's corridors.
An empty one.

*   *   *

Opening them, which required considerable effort,
Robert found himself not in a corridor at all, but lying

on a bed under a plastic canopy. Wires and tubes were connected all over him. His limbs felt leaden. With difficulty, he raised his right hand and pushed at the covering. It would not give. Then it struck him. The crystal – where was it, after all this? Looking down, he saw his left hand, curled into a fist, felt something hard inside it. Opening his fingers, Robert saw what it was: a small black coal.

Suddenly, a lot of the confidence drained out of him. He had been through so much, for so long, for this... Things would be much more difficult without the crystal. Still, he had only a short time to find Jane and escape. He looked outside at the round room, beds on the circumference, pointing at the centre, and saw himself there, under the glowing, flowing pyramid.

Nothing happened. Frustrated, he increased his concentration, putting all his effort into it. At last he moved. Lethargically, he picked himself off the floor and stood, dazed and weak between the beds. He felt as though he had the world's worst hangover. He was swaying and dizzy, put a hand out to steady himself. Four, no two of the beds were occupied. One held an old man. The other, Jane!

He staggered over to it and beat on the cover. "Jane!" he yelled. "Wake up!" After a few seconds, Jane opened her eyes lazily. A couple of intravenous tubes were leading into her arms, covered with bandages where they entered. She looked groggy and drugged; half seemed to recognise him, opened her lips, mouthed his name and a few words. Her eyes opened and closed again. She was losing consciousness. The cover was too strong. It would not budge. Robert could hardly keep upright himself. He fell to his knees, pulling with weaker and failing tugs.

Steps echoed behind him. He turned.

"The crystal" said McGee. "Where is it?"

Robert stayed silent. He had nothing to say. His head felt as though it was going to explode. He stared at the two McGees in front of him. Kneeling on the floor in only a pair of shorts, he felt vulnerable, started shivering. It was very cold.

The McGees stepped forward and hit out at his left hand. More pain. The coal shot out onto the floor. McGee scrambled for it. "You BLOODY FOOL!" he exclaimed in a barrage of spit.

A sound of running feet reached him. More faces appeared in the doorway and came into the room. McGee turned to Caroline, holding out the coal. "He tried to bring it back himself. I told him to call me, but he tried to bring it back himself." His face a snarl, he turned back and gave Robert a well-aimed kick in the stomach. Robert doubled up.

This situation was deteriorating rapidly. If he didn't get out now he never would. Mustering the last of his mental resources, Robert tried to think of a place he could be safe, lie down and recover. Calderstones Park, Liverpool: a dozen images flitted through his mind. He tried to grab one, hold it steady, fit the pyramid over it. All the while his reflexes were tensing, ready for another kick. Cuthbert and Caroline were talking loudly. Ananda began to argue.

*   *   *

Then quiet. He was lying on grass, feeling like death warmed up, but not much. The park came in and out of focus. Robert closed his eyes and lost consciousness.

He woke in what felt like early morning, coughing hard and shivering. It was still freezing cold. Rain drizzled down on his goosepimpled skin. The sun was up, behind clouds. No-one else was. Soon, no doubt, there would be a few joggers. Robert began limping towards the shelter of some chestnut trees.

He sat against a tree until the park began to get more populated, then started for the Allerton Road shops. On the way, he asked a well-manicured lady dog walker the date. She gave him a suspicious look and told him: August 22nd. God, that was close. There was only one day left. At least he would not be destitute long. How soon before the police started looking for him, though? Robert got to Oxfam via backstreets just after nine, attracting many a stare on the way.

His luck was in. The ladies on the counter listened to his tale of woe with sympathy. He told them he was homeless and broke, which was true. Could they lend him some clothes? He left in old shoes, trousers, shirt and jacket. His face was covered with a thin beard. Luckily the rain shower had left him relatively clean. After that, he walked four miles into town and sat, dozing in front of *Scientific American* in the Central Library until noon. By now he was feeling better, but terribly hungry. He found a few drunks outside on a bench and asked them if there was a free soup kitchen anywhere. One offered him a bottle of sherry as if that was nourishment enough. Gratefully, in a spirit of camaraderie, he accepted a swig.

"The Haris mate. Willyasham sware." He didn't know what time they came.

Robert thanked the man, wandered around a little, and went to sit amongst the shoppers and pensioners in Williamson Square. It had stopped raining and the sun was out. He read a few discarded tabloids to pass the time. Nothing on him yet.

The stalls and shops began to close down. At last the Playhouse taxi rank began to move. People were passing hurriedly to catch their buses. An old van drove up onto the pavement and stopped in the square's centre. The driver's door opened and a saffron-robed monk got out and went round the back. On the side was a hand-painted sign: 'Hare Krishna Food for life' with a with a red-and-yellow striped rising sun motif. Robert stood up and joined the motley bunch beginning to assemble by the van.

The monk assembled a folding table and put some buckets and paper plates on it. He began to serve out the food, chatting to the regulars. Robert got a plate of vegetables and rice, and a cup of juice. He sat down to eat it, then went back for some more. It tasted great, perhaps because he was so hungry.

That night, not caring to stay in the city centre, he slept in Sefton park, a shorter walk than Calderstones. Next morning dawned – the twenty-third – and he spent the day in much the same way until evening. *It* was due at seven o'clock.

At six forty-five, he was stationed, waiting on a corner in eyesight of the Duke Street warehouse. Not that he expected it early – he was just impatient and without a timepiece.

At seven exactly, it appeared. If Alistair had been furious about the Xthanite crystal, he was going to be bloody livid now. Robert hoped Jane would be all right. All the teleport machine equipment materialised, on a side street beside the car hire depot. He glanced around carefully, crossed over, and stroked his hand over the machine's parts. Touching a few switches, he took a headset and put it on.

"Location Ujelang Atoll, Pacific Ocean. Jump, confirm jump."

Again the street was empty.

<u>15</u> RETROSPECT

Hazily, Jane realised that she was waking up. Her body felt exhausted, but still, little by little, she was gaining consciousness. Where had she been? Where was she? Turning back and forth, she tried to put off the answers by keeping her eyes shut.

A memory, or dream, surfaced. Robert was shouting her name, standing over her, beating on a cover like a cage, trying to help her. It didn't seem to make much sense.

Wearily she opened her eyes, rubbed them with the back of a hand. Disoriented. Dazed. This wasn't Ingolstadt. A whole set of jumbled memories started running about her brain. She propped herself up and looked around. The noise had stopped. For six months solid, except for that day-trip to Ios, she had lived with that low soft humming. Now it wasn't there. The room was somewhere else, too. By the features, more like part of an old Victorian house. Windows looked up onto grass and flowerbeds. Barred on the outside. She was in a basement. Prison.

The door opened. In walked a familiar figure. Familiar from where? Female, fortyish, plainly dressed.

" 'Morning Jane. How are we today? Fancy a coffee and something to eat?"

Jane was dumbstruck. She coughed hoarsely.

"Right. Coffee, toast and a nice boiled egg. OK?" Jane stared blankly. More memories. No, it couldn't possibly... "Just lift your arm a second. There. That didn't hurt a bit, did it?" The woman had quickly and expertly turned back the sheets on her bed and injected her in the arm with a hypodermic. She felt numb and sick. Noticed (irrelevantly?) she was wearing a revolting peach nightdress she had never seen before.

"Wha.. Where, do I know you from?" she managed.

The woman smiled brightly. "Don't you remember me? I'm Mary. We worked together."

"But..."

"Don't worry. I'll send the Professor in shortly. He'll explain everything."

Jane's mind started to turn somersaults. She was back at Brookview hospital, but wasn't she a prisoner of the Illuminati? If this was Rob's doing, then he must be... where? How could Professor Heisenberg possibly be linked with the Illuminati when she met him long before any teleport stuff?

"But..." Mary left, soon returning with the Professor.

"Morning, Jane. Good to see you're back with us again. How're you feeling?"

"I'm tired... I don't know... Why am I here? And where's Robert?"

"Hmm. you've been under sedation for quite a while. You've had a breakdown. I'm afraid you're suffering from acute schizophrenia. A complex delusional system of delusional paranoia. I've put you on a course of Diazapan for the moment to stop your violent fits."

Jane's eyes grew large. Her mouth opened in disbelief. "I said, what have you done with Robert?"

"You didn't say that at all, actually," corrected the Professor. "Your brother is probably at home at the moment, recovering from your attack on him at his place of work."

Jane tried to sit up straighter, wanted to get out of bed, but could not. Her muscles were wasted with exhaustion.

"Let me phone him then," she demanded.

"I'm afraid that's not possible. It was he who requested that you be sectioned. I'm sorry, but he's had enough of you ringing him at all hours of the day and night with these fantasies about teleport machines and secret conspiracies. Young lady, you have a very vivid and fertile imagination."

Jane struggled to speak. Her confidence was faltering. She was getting steadily more confused and fuzzy. "You're lying. You're one of them. You're lying and you can't prove a thing."

"After you were subdued," said the Professor, "your brother took you home and found that you had completely wrecked your flat. Look at the pictures if you don't believe me." He tossed a packet on to the bed. As if they could prove *anything*.

ARJUNA KRISHNA-DAS

PART THREE
SUNDANCE

O son of Kunti, either you will be killed on the battlefield and attain the heavenly planets, or you will conquer and enjoy the earthly kingdom. Therefore, get up with determination and fight.

Krishna, Bhagavad-Gita 2.37

1   ATOLL ORDER

The island's most prominent attributes were: that it was uninhabited by other humans, isolated, hot, and had its own food and water supply. Generally the ideal sort of place should one, for example, wish to hide from an inter-planetary mafia for the next sixty years or so. There was also a higher-than-normal level of background radiation from French hydrogen bombe tests, but this seemed to bother the indigenous plant and animal population no more than it did Robert, who quite honestly had far more pressing and urgent matters on his mind.

The basic problems of survival were quite easily solved. Fruit, coconuts, fish and fresh water were readily available, as was shelter – in the caves beyond the lagoon and the jungley forest behind the beach. Above the lagoon was a small rocky hill. A coral reef, encircling the island, and visible at low tide, would have made landing a boat difficult. All told, Robert had about two square miles to himself.

For a week, he rested, recuperated and tried to relax. He did not attempt to use the mental teleport siddhi, fearing control or detection by the eye. Perhaps he did not even possess the power any more. Instead, he began to refine the teleport machine's software, making it work faster, and on a higher frequency. Less detectable. For power, he stole solar generators from an electronics company in Tokyo.

His small lab nestled under flapping canvas and swaying palm trees, the fractaerial aiming at the heavens, like the den of some castaway radio ham. For a while, Robert considered acquiring a revolver, then dismissed the thought – a gun would be crude, nasty, cheap. Now he knew what he was up against, there was ample reason to re-program Oliver for offensive capabilities. More subtle, flexible and powerful by far. He should have done this right from the start. Those had been days of innocence, naïveté.

At last ready, he sent flying TV cameras over Tibet's rugged and beautiful landscape, searching for Ingolstadt. A day and a half's concentrated staring at a bank of televisions left him stupefied and frustrated. Trying to keep track of the data from all five cameras was no mean feat, even under ideal conditions. The blazing, tropical heat and his underlying sense of panic were not. In a moment's detached resignation, the thought hit him. Of course! The teleport machine would have logged its start position in the flight to Liverpool. He could have got them there and then. Cursing, he turned to the console and issued commands to the computer.

Moments later, a solitary camera was rushing over the bleakly elevated landscape of the Kashmiri Himalayas. Not

Tibet at all. Robert gulped at the awesome perfection of the scene and adjusted the television's contrast. The transmitter was time compressing the signal, and bouncing it a thousand different ways to avoid detection. Silent peaks, spires and rooftops of the world, reflected in lakes of pure stillness. The view topped a crag and stopped, as Robert's finger lifted from the mouse.

"My God" he said, suddenly struck by a chill wholly alien to Ujeland Atoll. Amidst the features of Zajibal Gali was – a gap. A square-cut section right out of the mountain. Ingolstadt, which had been there – he recognised the view and the glacier – was gone. "Where the hell do you hide half a mountain?" asked Robert of a large and hairy spider crawling up his left arm. He shook the creature off, recalled the camera and powered down the equipment.

It was another day – spent fishing, fire and shelter making – before Robert decided on his next move. He had to stay on the offensive in order not to feel like prey. He was already feeling bad enough about Jane as it was. If it had not been for him, her life would not be in danger. The heat enforced in him an uncharacteristic slowness in action and thought. Not dull, but reflective, self-analytical. Philosophical even. Robert found himself asking difficult questions. Not just about what to do next, but why he was in this ridiculous situation at all. What had he been trying to achieve with teleportation in the first place? It was not just a question of keeping the technology from the Arabs, not just the pursuit of knowledge. When it came right down to it, he had to admit, it was the sense of power that was driving him. Power over nature, of himself, over others. Was that it? Yes.

And yet in another sense he felt powerless. Where had all this got him?

Restless and impatient, feeling he had to do *something*, Robert decided to retrace Jane's last steps.

First to Delhi, to the teleport shack. Hopeless. The place was inhabited by what seemed to be three or four large families, only a few of whom spoke the most rudimentary English. No-one, nowhere else in India presented itself to him as a fruitful avenue of investigation.

Disguised, he hoped, behind large black sunglasses, and hair permed and dyed a curly red, Robert returned to Liverpool. He knew only a couple of Jane's friends, by first name only. Much less how to find them. In fact, the only one he knew how to find was Dave.

*   *   *

Anger is usually an emotion which, under the right circumstances, is not difficult to summon up. Jane was seething, or rather trying to seethe. All she actually felt, thanks to the Diazapan, was tired. The nearest she had come to hitting someone was when Margaret had tried to involve her in 'non-confrontational' group therapy with the lunatics. So, as a result, she was back down here, sitting alone most of the time except for a head round the door every quarter hour, asking her how she felt. Mostly, she did not even reply. All she could do was send her head round in circles, trying to work out how the Professor could possibly be doing the Illuminati's dirty work, and how she could get out.

Mary had only just finished one of these little checks on her when Ananda materialised in the other easy chair. Jane blinked. She would have reached for the nurse-call button by the bed, but she was too flabbergasted.

"What now, Bitch?" she asked, getting straight to the point.

Ananda admired her perfect fingernails. She flashed a business-like smile at Jane. "We thought you might have some questions. The others had no objection to my coming to tell you a few things, and I thought the satisfaction might make up somewhat for all our inconvenience."

"What inconvenience?" asked Jane. "Bitch!"

"Relocation, stick insect. Of Ingolstadt."

"Well, I haven't. I'd get straighter answers out of Robert's cat. A creature with far greater standards of humanity than the lot of you put together." The indictment left Jane exhausted. She slumped in her chair.

"That's OK," said Ananda. "I understand your feelings."

Jane snorted.

"But I'm going to tell you anyway. To start with, you may have noticed that Alistair likes information. Lots of it. We're plugged into more than you can imagine. The computer picked out you and Robert years ago as worth watching. Not only are you closely related. After statistical analysis, it identified both of you as being on the crest of leading edge trends." Jane stifled an "Oh", but let an eyebrow rise involuntarily before she could stop it. "We made sure that Robert had all the facilities he needed. As for you, we just watched, and made sure you stayed in a suitable environment. You were provided with subliminal suggestions to apply for work here. So was the Professor, to employ you. As for his present delusions, they are false memories implanted last week at a medical conference he never got to."

Jane avoided looking at Ananda, stared out of the window.

"Expect a visit from your dear brother soon. I'm sure he's out of his mind with worry about you. We'll be waiting. Oh, is that the time? I must go. You will tell the Professor about my little visit, won't you? I'm sorry I can't stay longer to say hello to him. Bye."

She left, leaving behind an unpleasant smell of cologne.

As Mary put her head round the door again, Jane barely moved. The bait was being played with, but it wouldn't join in. No. She would find a way. Get away. Warn Robert. Somehow or other.

*   *   *

The Health store was deserted. Robert took the sunglasses off and cleared his throat. After some time, he cleared it again, rather loudly, and began to wonder whether he should go behind the counter and look in the back room. He was just edging round to peer through the doorway surreptitiously when the front door opened to admit a rather scruffy-looking man. Robert found himself in the embarrassing position of being behind the counter of a shop with no staff, the contents of which he knew nothing about, except that you could eat them. If you were a rabbit, that was. This guy looked more like a local vagrant than a customer. Perhaps he would just look around and go away. Dave should be pleased with him for looking after the place.

The man looked down and coughed, with difficulty. Robert felt sorry for him. Perhaps he had come to beg some food. The man spoke. "Err... I wonder can I get you anything?"

Robert scratched his unfamiliar curls of hair. "You mean do I want any jobs doing, errands run? No, no, it's OK. Really, I don't need anything today."

"Then, err... you're just looking round?" asked the man.

Robert realised that this was Dave and flushed. He stepped away from the counter and put a hand out to shake. "I'm sorry. You must be Dave. I'm Robert Ashley, Jane's brother." Dave looked relieved, and shook Robert's hand damply.

"Good to meet you, Rob. What can I do for you?"

"Well, she's gone missing and I'm not sure where to start looking."

"Hmm." Dave's brow knitted in thought as he pulled the cellophane off a packet of tobacco. Frowning, he began to roll a cigarette. "I've not seen her myself for, oh, six or seven months – January it was. Debbie and Rick too, they've not seen her. I know, 'cause they've asked me. Smoke?"

Robert shook his head and opened a small spiral-bound notebook. "No thanks." He scribbled the names down.

"Actually it's quite worrying, I suppose," said Dave, getting into his element now. "I mean one minute she's herself again, running this Lakshmi Trading all over the place, all bright and breezy. The next – she's gone. Just this strange note." He lit his roll-up and bent down behind the counter, began rifling through a box of old envelopes and scraps of paper. "Here it is." He held it up between them.

To all customers and suppliers of Lakshmi Trading

We are sorry to announce our immediate closure due to unforeseen circumstances. Hoping you can make alternative arrangements.

yours etc.

"Doesn't reveal much, does it?" said Dave. Robert agreed. It was a good deal more terse than his departure notes. A dead end.

"So where do you think I should look next?"

"Well, this was posted from India. I suppose she's over there somewhere. Maybe Goa."

"What about –" Robert looked at his notebook "– Debbie and Rick?"

"I can give you Debbie's address. Rick, I don't know. Here." Dave took the notepad and scribbled in it. "Well, good luck. Let me know if you find her. Tell her to get in touch."

"Thanks," said Robert. "I will."

He bade Dave goodbye and left. Debbie lived nearby, off Lark Lane. The walk took five minutes or so. He had not found a lot out from Dave, but it was a start. The path to Debbie's house was a tunnel of leafy branches. He fought his way through and tapped on the front door's window, which was loose and broken.

A dog started barking, followed half a minute later by steps. A man in his early twenties opened the door, kindly looking, wearing dreadlocks, blue T-shirt and jeans. He held a pink guitar lead in his hand, one plug half-soldered on.

"Debbie? Yeah, come up."

Robert followed, squeezing past speaker cabinets the size of a small car. He felt his way up the stairs and through the doors of the flat.

"Deb, someone to see you."

Debbie closed her book and looked up. "Hello." She was older than – Pete, that was his name, he remembered now. Forever sweeping long brown hair out of her face, she wore a mauve blouse over khaki leggings, and seemed to be staring slightly above him, which was disconcerting.

"I'm Robert, Jane's brother" he began, realising what she was looking at. "Oh, my hair – I dyed it," he explained.

Debbie seemed to relax somewhat, and offered him a seat next to hers on the sofa. Pete was crouched over his cables by the window, next to a tall speaker, quietly pumping out bass-heavy reggae.

"She's disappeared, hasn't she?" said Debbie. "Do you know where she is?"

"I'm afraid I don't," said Robert. "I was hoping we could come up with some ideas together." He sat on the edge of the seat feeling vaguely uncomfortable.

"She's been gone a long time," said Debbie. Between the lines, she was saying 'Where were you six months ago?' "hasn't she?"

Robert improvised. "All she said to me was that she was going away for a bit. Wouldn't tell me where. 'Course I was worried, but what could I do? She's an adult, isn't she?"

Debbie looked away, fidgeting about for a cigarette. Finally she lit one and inhaled. "If you ask me she was all right 'till she got that job at the mental home. Sounded like a very weird place to me. That's where she was cracking up. I'd ask there if I were you."

A stone hit the window. Robert jerked. His bowels turned to water. Pete rattled the window up, said a few words and threw some keys down.

"Brookview hospital?" asked Robert
Debbie nodded. "Yeah."

2   BATTLE OF WHERE

Lime Street station is a large, anonymous space. It is busy, but not so crowded on a normal day. Robert figured it probably the safest place to phone from. Nervously, he crossed the concourse, looking up at a huge billboard advertisement for his old employers – 'leaders in telecommunications'.

Considering carefully, he looked up. There was something unnerving about Debbie's lead. As if she could sense a sinister connection. Whatever it was... some women had that ability. He realised he was more than nervous. He was frightened. There would be only one chance to get this right.

And then the answer walked right up to him. A student, obviously. Just the job. " 'Scuse me," said Robert. "I wonder if you could help. I need someone to make a phone call for me, that's all. Here -" he fished in his wallet – "A fiver now, another one after you've made the call." He passed him the note, together with a phonecard. The student looked bemused, puzzled, as if he had come across a fool, giving money away like this.

"Yeah, OK," he agreed.

"Tell them your name is Robert Ashley." Robert explained who to call, what he should say, and told him to come up to the bar overlooking the concourse for the rest of his money. They parted, and Robert quickly went up and found a seat by the window. By the time he got there, he could see the youth already talking in a phone booth opposite. Then he stopped talking. He seemed to be on hold. He looked at his watch a few times, and up at the bar's dark smoked glass windows, as if this had not been such a good idea after all. After a minute or so he was reconnected and began talking again. He turned his back. Then Robert noticed four policemen converging on him, spread out, walking swiftly towards their prey. When close enough, they ran, truncheons out, and leapt at him, pinning his body to the ground, beating his torso and arms. It was as he had feared. There was no protection, even in the most open and public places. He was a marked man, alone against the world. Robert turned a ghostly shade of white, made for the gents, and vanished.

*　　　　*　　　　*

In this room, an inmate was tearing up paper and eating it. The next was a smart TV lounge. Bodies, their minds elsewhere, were slumped, rolling, rocking and lying in front of a large-screen Australian soap. Impatiently, he pushed the joystick. A nurse, adjusting her lipstick in a bathroom; three more empty rooms: that was it. Robert cursed. He must have missed her, but it was only minutes since his proxy phone call. He took a few deep breaths, and began again from the top; paused on the professor in his study, dictating a rambling, obtuse speech to Miss Dwight, scribbling in her spiral-bound note book. He continued and noticed a cupboard door beneath the stairs. Downstairs again. Here was another room. And here was Jane.

Robert felt simultaneously exhilarated and terrified. Fate had granted him one more chance to rescue his sister. He doubted there would be another.

Checking the room from all angles, and Jane in close-up – she was sitting, staring into space out of the high window – Robert took his weapons and checked them. One was fashioned from a TV remote control, the other a video game gun. He placed the gun inside a jacket pocket and adjusted his earpiece; then, stealing himself for the worst, pressed the handset button that would take him there.

*   *   *

"Ahgh!" cried out Jane in shock.

"Stand behind me. Quick!" said Robert. Dizzily, she got up and obeyed.

"Thank God you've come."

Robert was jerking his head this way and that, all over the room. Hardly glancing at her, he thrust the toy gun into her hand. "Watch yourself with that. There's no safety catch," he warned.

Disoriented, she put her free left arm around his chest. "I was so... I, I knew you'd come."

"Where are they?!" asked Robert desperately. It was too much to expect an effortless escape.

"She came, before," said Jane.

"Who?"

"Ananda"

There was no point waiting around for something bad to happen. Robert pressed the button that should have taken them back to the Atoll, via a million intermediate points.

"Hey, what's happened?" said Jane. She sounded strange, nearly as scared as he was.

"Just a sec.' The machine was speaking to him, in an inflectionless female voice. "Sorry. Destination beam error. Sorry. Destination beam..." He shut it off. The silence was eerie, total.

Their surroundings... well, there were was nothing there surrounding them, a dull gloom, but no colour, nothing to focus on, like a mist, but... nothing as definite as that.

"Where are we?" asked Jane. She clutched him tighter, as if afraid of falling away into the featureless void.

"Don't worry, I'm still here," he said. "I think we're stuck between two tele-points.

"How stuck?"

Robert was about to say 'not very', when, appropriately, they began to move forward. At least it felt like moving. The sensation was like accelerating in a fast car. But there was no wind, no visual clue, still no sound.

Protectively, he put an arm around her. Dimly, as if through clouds, streaks of light were appearing. Short lines of brilliance rushing past them. The G-force increased until it ceased to be a pleasant, thrilling sensation and began to be painful. Their faces distorted as skin rippled back, flapping, the only noise in an otherwise silent wind.

261

The streaks of light lengthened, sharp white on black, without end. Robert wanted to speak, ask how Jane was, but, afraid his jaw would be torn off, did not try. It was becoming harder to swallow, more and more uncomfortably painful. His whole body felt as if it was being torn apart. They clung tighter in vacant fear.

Then, just at the moment he could bear it no longer, everything began to spin around them.

"Where are we?" asked Robert to himself. He was being pulled apart from Jane, felt her fingers clutching at his arm, his hand, and then she was gone, shot away from him like a bullet. At the same time, the tearing forces stopped.

"Jane!" he called. There was an echo or reply, he could not tell which. He was still turning, floating in a way which might have been pleasant in other circumstances.

He tried to focus on his surroundings again. God, it was difficult. What was turning? him? or.. millions of coloured dots moving across his vision. He blinked, and they seemed to be moving a different way.

"Jane!" Where was she?

The dots were making up a picture, he was sure. If he could only focus on it... They swam into coherence. For a split second, a huge crystalline sphere.. like a planet seen from above.. then dissolved again. It was the same visual field. His brain was just unable to process the sensory input from his eyes. It was frustrating beyond endurance. And he dared not teleport anywhere without her. Even if he could.

"Jane!!" Where was he? In all the miserable far flung God forsaken hell holes of outer hyperspace? Where was this? He flicked open a flap on the remote control. "Jane! Come in, Jane. Where are you?"

A voice crackled back through the speaker.

"Ahhh. I'm.. Where we.. Where we.." It broke up in bursts of static. "the lab.. fractaerial.. where.. fix the.. Rob.. we headed? Where?"

A cold sweat broke out all over Rob's body. The dots were swimming before his eyes maddeningly. He was a hair's breadth away from losing Jane's signal. He ought to tell her the location or she might be lost forever in..

"Where's the fractaerial?" crackled the speaker.

"Where's the fractaerial?" asked a voice in his brain. "Where's the fractaerial?" "Where's the fractaerial?" The pressure was really getting to him.

"It's on the I," he began. The Eye. Who wanted to know anyhow? The Eye?

"Help me, Rob. Help me!" cried Jane's voice through the speaker.

"I'm trying, damn you!" he shouted.

Robert pushed a combination of keys, attempting to locate her.

There was a quiet sound, like a bell or gong, trembling in and out of audibility. Feeling a cold blast of air on the back of his neck, he turned, horrified to encounter a huge and hideous looking reptile. His weapon raised, it roared, jaws and claws raised over him. He closed his finger on the trigger key.

"Rob! It's Me!" shouted Jane, simultaneously as he pressed it. The creature lurched for his arm, swinging the weapon away; he chopped its neck with the side of his hand.

"Ow!" screamed Jane. He felt her hair, her ear. Blinked. She stood before him, rubbing the bruise.

"Christ" said Robert. "I almost atomised you. Sorry."

"You would too if I hadn't pushed your arm away. What's going on?"

"I can't see straight."

"What, all these bloody dots? I can't either. I can see you though."

Suddenly a woman's voice boomed loudly around them. "Where's the fractaerial, Robert?" An area of dots seemed to bulge out with every word.

"Come and find out, Bitch!" responded Jane. The effort exhausted her. She closed her eyes, head swaying, and put it on Robert's chest. Her legs and torso rose, pointing out horizontally from him.

"Jane! Wake up!" he snapped, trying to shake her shoulders. This shook him as much as it did her. The indeterminately coloured and sized dots halted in their movement, then glided off in another direction.

Jane blinked and opened her eyes again, trying to orient herself into a sensible position. "Ugh.." she moaned. "Watch out!"

Robert turned his head, tried to twist his body. It was Cuthbert Jennings, still in the same ruffled white shirt and blue jeans. He tossed his head back and laughed. His golden hair splayed out as if in shock. First left, then right, he began to twist his arms around himself like a madman, still laughing. Then he let go of what he had been holding on to. A pair of springs, weighted at the ends, unravelled themselves, flying round him. He became encircled by flashing, glinting razor strips. Their very sound was sharp. His body was swaying back and forth, faster and faster in reaction to the movements of his arms. The blades glinted and shone, whistling and whooping. They were reflecting light from somewhere hidden; all he could see was dull and diffused through the grainy dots. It was like being too close to a newspaper picture.

"Where's the fractaerial, Robert?" the voice boomed again. The speaker was unfamiliar, the question becoming tedious.

"I gave it to you," he said. "Can't you look after anything?"

Jane's fingers dug into his arms. Cuthbert and his sphere of swishing blades were advancing on them. Vainly, Robert waved a free hand, trying to push them back against nothing. "Tsk," he tutted, pressing a button on the handset. For a few moments, they retreated, then Cuthbert laughed louder as he realised what they were doing, and began to close the gap.

Jane raised her gun and fired. There was a strange noise, like the sound of an orchestra tuning up in free fall, compressed into a second and played backwards. Cuthbert split up into hundreds of cubes, as if he had been through a cheese wire mesh. Each cube was bouncing within one great invisible cube twenty feet long. Some held a writhing section of limb, a square of shirt, jean or trainer, others, a length of razor spring. As the little cubes zipped about, bouncing off the sides of the larger one, they sometimes hit one another. Each collision made a small explosion, then the collided blocks vanished. Gradually, the random explosions died down, as the remains of Cuthbert disintegrated.

"Beautiful!" said Jane, sniggering.

"Good shot!" said Robert.

Before they could catch their breath, another assailant appeared. Dressed exactly like Cuthbert, a different face, but, horribly, the same manic grin. He threw his head back and laughed, sounding almost identical. Before either had a chance to move, he began to circle them swiftly on all sides, in an exact copy of the way he was now swinging the blades. Too fast to follow.

"Christ!" said Jane. "It's the guy in the phonebox."

Robert was madly waving his handset about, vainly trying to follow their new assailant's locus. "What phonebox?" he asked.

Jane held her gun out, shut her eyes and squeezed the trigger. A moment later, the backwards compressed tuning-up noise vibrated again as their foe was reduced to bouncing and exploding cubes.

"In Cuthbert's lab!" she explained. "Look out! Here's another one!"

The greeting this time was colder, shorter, as another Cuthbert clone nodded with malice before them. Even before raising his head he exploded into a rainbow of shimmering dust.

"Oops!" said Robert. "I shouldn't keep that button pressed down so long. It might melt the fractaerial." Suddenly he grimaced, and clasped his left arm. His shirt was ripped, and the flesh beneath was bleeding profusely.

Ahead of them, another Cuthbert-clothed figure was receding rapidly into the distance.

Robert transferred the handset into his left hand, still using his right to press hard on the wound.

"They're learning," said Jane.

It vanished to almost a dot, then began to grow again, veering from side to side, round, up and down in a randomly varying course.

"Here," said Robert. "I'll put it on wide field. That'll slow him down, then you can stiff him." He tapped a few keys, then held the unit out, button pressed at the approaching menace.

266

Nothing seemed to be stopping it. In seconds they would be sliced meat. Jane screamed, as the razor ribbons cut into her near field of vision. Then, to a deepening raspberry-like noise, the figure abruptly and jerkily de-accelerated, step by step, finally jerking to a halt a mere six feet in front of them.

"That's what I call a close shave," said Jane, raising her gun. This time the figure was older, much older, endlessly wrinkled, almost completely degenerate. All the same, his arms were held out, the deadly razor springs stretching from them, impotently. He looked at them with an expression of pure hatred, moving painfully slowly, in sudden jumps as if caught in digital treacle, which, in a sense, he was.

"The old man in the cryogenic lab?" mused Robert.

"C. Jennings stroke CNS" said Jane "You only live twice." And with that, she stiffed him.

3   DISEMBODIED, DISMEMBERED

Jane watched with satisfaction as dismembered cubes of the late and hopefully final Cuthbert Jennings bounced, exploding all around them. Whether it was the length of time since her last injection or just an adrenaline buzz, she was definitely not feeling tired any more. Rather the reverse.

"Back to back! Quick!" she shouted at Robert. He got the idea straight away, and turned, somehow managing to lock an uninjured elbow round one of her own.

Suddenly there was a blast of light so bright it hurt her eyes, like a whole sky of suns. Immediately, she closed them. Was the Eye throwing atom bombs now? Surely they couldn't be that mad about losing Cuthbert? Then she realised two things in quick succession:

1. Either the Eye were unbelievably bad shots, or, more probably, they were not throwing atom bombs *at* them at all.

2. It was not an atom bomb, at least not like one she had heard of in all her days as a Youth CND facilitator. She could tell this by the dull red flashes through her eyelids. Atom bombs did not do this. It was more like a strobe followed by your body being sucked off its skeleton by a red-hot wind at a thousand miles an hour.

Before this reasoning had a chance to develop, the sound began. It was very deep and far too loud. It would have been far too loud at any volume, but was especially so at this one. She felt weak and sick, like jelly all over.

"Rob, what's going on?" Strangely, she did not have to shout. She could hear her voice, though shaky, quite clearly.

"Pressure and electromagnetic wave warfare. Shut your eyes, press the trigger and wave that gun in front of you. It's on wide beam already."

Through a fog of pain and confusion, she did it. Her frame felt delicate, mortally weakened. The effort of waving the gun was torture. Put it down though, and they would both be dead. A vision flashed through her mind, of clinging on to life by her fingertips.

The flashes were dying away. Nervously, she half-opened her right eye, peering through lashes. It was Alistair. He was in combat fatigues, ammo belt draped round his waist.

"Where's the fractaerial, Robert?" boomed the voice again. This time, it was unmistakably Ananda.

Robert stayed silent amidst the noise. She could feel him clasp her arm tighter.

"Your sister won't stand much more of this, you know. Is your precious toy worth more to you than her?"

Jane tried to raise the gun, point it. It wouldn't move. Drop it, she thought. Let go, float away. Alistair held up something to his mouth, biting it, then threw. It flew. This time, her eyes shut in time. Even so, the light hurt.

"You OK?" she managed.

"Yeah. It's all on your side. I've got Ananda here with some kind of sound gun. What about you?"

"Alistair. Yeah, I'm OK." But she wasn't. It was the mind machine. She knew it. The deep pulsing crackle was tearing through her. She felt torn open.

"Maybe she'll go mad again before she dies, Robert."

The light flashes were blending with the sound. It was mixing up. If she shut her mouth, would the sound stop? Maybe it was coming from within her.

"Where's the teleport machine?" He didn't answer. He wasn't dead; he was gripping her. The sound was going up and down; or was it her? The lights were making colours and patterns on the inside of her eyelids. She opened her mouth to scream; her body retched in spasms of vomit. Ananda was demanding the fractaerial. Her voice was bouncing all over the place; wobbly, distorted. Jane still jerked. Her stomach was empty but the spasms wouldn't stop. All the sounds, everything was mixing up.

Then something gripped hard. All around her. It was Rob. She turned, felt covered all over with him. He was shouting in her ear. "Mirror! Got a Mirror!" Mirror? Yeah. She was wearing one. She pushed him and tore at her shirt. It was inside. The big ankh. He grabbed it, held it out, nearly strangling her. He was shouting again. She wanted to die, felt like she was close to having her wish granted. Every cell of her body was sending unbearable pain signals to her brain.

Then she realised, she was making the lights herself; opened her eyes. No more strobe, just the jelly-throb. Alistair had grown, like a giant, but impossibly thin, body waving in and out, then he swung ninety degrees, looked like a huge inflated stomach. His eyes were black, just sockets. He was reaching, grappling for another strobe-grenade.

"Shut your eyes!" shouted Rob. "Stiff him!" She felt for the gun on the end of her hand, raised it and somehow pulled the trigger.

Alistair was still there. Large as life, twice as ugly.. She couldn't understand. Her hand was hurting even more. She looked down. It seemed to be all muscle and bone. Blood and melted plastic. She screamed. Another strobe-flash exploded. Rob shook her. The sound was getting louder. "Fight it with your mind!" he yelled. "It's all we've got left!"

"Wabble fac fac tolible!" boomed Ananda.

"You can't kill me!" yelled Robert. "I'm not this body. Can't kill me, can't kill me!"

Like a playground taunt, she thought. "You can't kill me..", but death felt close, very close. Her body felt loose, disconnected "Can't kill.. can't, can't kill me.." She was losing touch, out of her mind with pain.

Then, out of pain altogether, like a film, she saw her life flash before her. Birth, nursery, school, birthdays, Christmases, forgotten friends. Even so, it had all been so short, so little. Every last thing was there: Boyfriends, Poly, jobs. Then Brookview, Rob and the teleport machine. India, Lakshmi trading, Delhi. Around her she could see a light, feel an overwhelming presence of love. Then an image of the devotee on the bus passed in front of her. A phrase stuck in her mind – *Hare Krishna, Hare Krishna...*

Rob was still screaming. "You can't kill me!"

Then the light blossomed. Out of silence, nothing like the strobe. All around. She felt drawn out, away to another realm.

"God, let me live!" she cried. Then suddenly the pain was back, not as bad, but...uncomfortable.

She opened her eyes. They were alive, panting in short breaths, holding on, hugging each other. Her ears rang. The pain was receding.

In front of them, Ananda was buzzing and crackling like a short circuit on a railway line, white-hot, limbs stretched out in shock. The sound gun lay, useless, at her side.

The dots dissolved, or merged into a scene as if it had never been hidden. Ananda, Alistair were gone. At their feet was a planet, vital, full of colour, sparkling like a gem. Over its horizon came a crack of light. Sun was rising. And above all this, a face. Disembodied, like the Cheshire Cat, with blonde hair plaited into a cone, beauty beyond belief. She smiled and winked.

Jane turned to Robert, floating at her side. She was about to ask who she was. He was mesmerised; probably would not hear her.

The scene dissolved again. She was falling, down and up at the same time. Through flashes of rainbow stars. Then they were standing on a hot beach. Jane collapsed on the sand.

4 WORLD OF POSSIBILITY

By the time she came to, it was evening. Beneath her was a bed of grass and leaves. A fire crackled contentedly, and behind it Robert, coughing and waving away the wood smoke. His shirt was torn, his arm bandaged. Fish were cooking on an arrangement of sticks and stones at the fire's base. Above, the moon shone amidst a numinous backdrop of stars. Jane just watched for a while, silent, simply glad to be alive and free. Her eyes blinked open and closed.

"So, we beat them, huh?" she called.

Robert looked over, startled. "Yeah, I think we had a little help. Someone up there likes us." He raised his eyes to heaven.

"God?" Jane was incredulous.

"A friend. *Parija*. Didn't you see her?"

"Oh, *her*. Yeah." She wiped her mouth. There was no sick. Robert must have washed it. "Got any water?" He had. She drank luxuriously from the tumbler. "Where are we?"

Robert turned the fish over with a stick. "Ujelang Atoll. Middle of the Pacific Ocean."

"Why?"

"I thought it would be a good place to get away from them."

"Oh." She got up off her elbow and walked round the fire. Her body, especially her right hand, felt pretty rough. Not as rough as they'd almost been. She leant on a tree.

Quite soon, Robert considered the fish done. Jane kindly thanked him for the offer, but sat munching a bunch of bananas while he filleted and consumed his catch.

"You'll get the shits eating just fruit."

She shrugged. "You'll grow scales. Anyhow, why can't you get food from off the island?"

Robert did not answer, just sat chewing, poking at the fire.

"The teleport machine's bust, isn't it."

He swallowed, with difficulty. "Just the fractaerial. It melted. I was afraid it might. You see, it was only designed for short bursts of power, not as a weapon."

Jane threw another banana skin into the fire. It shrank and turned black. "Never mind. It's only a machine."

Robert looked shocked. "Don't think machines don't have souls. Mine have hearts too."

She laughed. Was he serious? Sometimes you could never tell. "Anyhow, what happened to you up on the moon? It looked like a pretty amazing place. In fact you looked rather strange."

Robert threw a few more sticks on the fire and found a tree he could lean against. "Remember that pyramid sacrifice in

Mu," he began, "you know, with all the bowing priests, and the inner pyramid about to explode. Well it did..."

Jane listened, increasingly spellbound, as Robert told her of his Chandralokan adventures. At Parija's mention of the Syamantaka jewel, her jaw dropped open. The *what?* As he continued, confirmation became certain. Gold drops! Robert's healing leg! Would that she could be so lucky. This was indeed the same jewel she had heard of on the way to Rajpur.

After his story had finished, Jane spoke of the Syamantaka jewel story she had heard from the Hare Krishna devotee on the bus.

"It's the same one, isn't it?" said Robert. They continued to talk, long into the night, as Jane recounted her experiences as a prisoner at Ingolstadt.

*   *   *

Jane explored the island, as Robert had done, but at greater length. She sat on small cliffs for long periods, looking out over the ocean. The clear water revealed a world of marine life, from tiny flashes of colour and pulsing jelly fish to ominous looking barracuda. Inland, the jungley forest held few surprises, but comparable beauty. While Robert sweated and swore over the equipment he was trying to repair, she paddled cautiously in the sea and went for long walks. At times, she hummed or sang – songs she tried to remember, or made up herself. Over the weeks, her skin was acquiring a tan, while Robert's inexplicably remained pale, or burnt red.

He was building in enthusiasm again while working. Now the Illuminati were finished, no-one could stop him. This time he would not be so easily out-manoeuvred. Already, Jane had noticed scrawled drafts of faxes to multinational companies, offering the secret of teletransportation – for a price.

Jane listened to his schemes without interest. She had heard it all before, was bored with it all. And the island? Not quite bored, but indifferent. It was good to be away from her captors, but... She still felt, in some inexpressible way, a yearning – for people, a still elusive freedom, a life beyond some temporary sensual happiness punctuated by problems.

Her hand was healing well under Robert's bandages, which he renewed and washed daily. The damage was not as bad as it had at first seemed. Her mind was plagued by uncertainty about the future. Inarticulated questions bobbed around her subconsciousness, dormant, as if through lack of stimulation. The only outside contact had been an occasional plane, miles up and away.

The days turned into weeks, passing uneventfully, without count.

"I've had enough!" she announced to Robert one afternoon. "I want to go back to civilisation."

He snorted slightly, stifling a laugh. "Where's that?"

"Don't. I'm going back. Maybe to Dave. Maybe check out that Hare Krishna thing." She had said it without realising, up to that point, what her plans were.

"Be my guest," said Robert. "There's no teleport."

"How're we going to get away then?"

"We?"

"You're not going to stay here for ever. Are you?"

He looked down and twisted a screwdriver in his hands. "I'm not going to repair it here."

"Don't bother repairing it at all," said Jane. "Look at all the trouble it's caused. Look what trouble it would be if you did make another one? What if everyone had one?"

Robert looked away. He was sad, too tired to argue right now. His fuzzy black beard made him look more like a computer boffin than ever. "My mystic siddhi's gone too," he complained." Jane felt sorry for him. "But I suppose I could cobble together a transmitter, and radio for help." He looked as though the task was beneath him.

*   *   *

The Cessna twin prop amphibian flew through a clear blue pacific sky it had to itself. A pilot and navigator were sitting at the controls, respectively flying and peering down through binoculars. Coming up was the westmost island of the Ujelang Atoll group. The plane banked to the right and descended, to circle the island's beach.

"There they are!" called the navigator. A hundred feet below, now behind, stood a man and a woman, hands up, waving in the air.

EPIL O GUE

... to Aquarius.

Vishnu opens his eyes once more. The fish has joined his cousins in the water. He blinks his eyes and lies back, in an ocean bubbling with universes ...

ANGELS CHÎC

Lightning Source UK Ltd.
Milton Keynes UK
UKOW03f0607130417
299019UK00001B/10/P